Italo Calvino

MR PALOMAR

Translated from the Italian by
William Weaver

published by Pan Books

First published 1983 by Giulio Einaudi editore s.p.a.
First published in Great Britain 1985 by Martin Secker & Warburg Ltd
This Picador edition published 1986 by Pan Books Ltd,
Cavaye Place, London SW10 9PG
9 8 7 6 5 4 3
© Giulio Einaudi editore s.p.a. 1983
ISBN 9 330 29092 4
Printed and bound in Great Britain by
Richard Clay (The Chaucer Press) Ltd, Bungay, Suffolk

CONTENTS

PALOMAR'S VACATION

PALOMAR ON THE BEACH

Reading a wave

The sea is barely wrinkled, and little waves strike the sandy shore. Mr Palomar is standing on the shore, looking at a wave. Not that he is lost in contemplation of the waves. He is not lost, because he is quite aware of what he is doing: he wants to look at a wave and he is looking at it. He is not contemplating, because for contemplation you need the right temperament, the right mood, and the right combination of exterior circumstances; and though Mr Palomar has nothing against contemplation in principle, none of these three conditions applies to him. Finally it is not "the waves" that he means to look at, but just one individual wave: in his desire to avoid vague sensations, he establishes for his every action a limited and precise object.

Mr Palomar sees a wave rise in the distance, grow, approach, change form and color, fold over itself, break, vanish, and flow again. At this point he could convince himself that he has concluded the operation he had set out to achieve, and he could go away. But it is very difficult to isolate one wave, separating it from the wave immediately following it, which seems to push it and at times overtakes it and sweeps it away; just as it is difficult to separate that one wave from the wave that precedes it and seems to drag it towards the shore, unless it turns against its follower as if to arrest it. Then if you consider the breadth of the wave, parallel to the shore, it is hard to decide where the advancing front extends regularly and where it is separated and segmented into independent waves, distinguished by their speed, shape, force, direction.

In other words, you cannot observe a wave without bearing in mind the complex features that concur in shaping it and the other, equally complex ones that the wave itself originates. These aspects vary constantly, so each wave is different from another wave, even if not immediately adjacent or successive; in other words there are some forms and sequences that are repeated, though irregularly distributed in space and time. Since what Mr Palomar means to do at this moment is simply to *see* a wave, that is, to perceive all its simultaneous components without overlooking any of them, his gaze will dwell on the movement of the wave that strikes the shore, until it can record aspects not previously perceived; as soon as he notices that the images are being repeated, he will know he has seen everything he wanted to see and he will be able to stop.

A nervous man who lives in a frenzied and congested world, Mr Palomar tends to reduce his relations with the outside world; and to defend himself against the general neurasthenia he tries to keep his sensations under control insofar as possible.

The hump of the advancing wave rises more at one point than at any other and it is here that it becomes hemmed in white. If this occurs at some distance from the shore, there is time for the foam to fold over upon itself and vanish again, as if swallowed, and at the same moment invade the whole, but this time emerging again from below, like a white carpet rising from the bank to welcome the wave that is arriving. But just when you expect that wave to roll over the carpet, you realize it is no longer wave but only carpet, and this also rapidly disappears, to become a glinting of wet sand that quickly withdraws, as if driven back by the expansion of the dry, opaque sand that moves its jagged edge forward.

At the same time the indentations in the brow of the wave must be considered, where it splits into two wings, one stretching towards the shore from right to left and the other from left to right, and the departure-point or the destination of their divergence or convergence is this negative tip, which follows the advance of the wings but is always held back, subject to their alternate overlapping until another wave, a stronger wave, overtakes it, with the same problem of divergence-convergence, and then a wave stronger still, which resolves the knot by shattering it.

Taking the pattern of the waves as model, the beach thrusts into the water some faintly-hinted points, prolonged in submerged sandy shoals, shaped and destroyed by the currents at every tide. Mr Palomar has chosen one of these low tongues of sand as his observation-point, because the waves strike it on either side, obliquely, and overrunning the half-submerged surface, they meet their opposites. So to understand the composition of a wave, you have to consider these opposing thrusts, which to some extent are counter-balanced and to some extent are added together, to produce a general shattering of thrusts and counter-thrusts in the usual spreading of foam.

Mr Palomar now tries to limit his field of observation; if he bears in mind a square zone of, say, ten meters of shore by ten meters of sea, he can carry out an inventory of all the wave-movements that are repeated with varying frequency within a given time-interval. The hard thing is to fix the boundaries of this zone, because if, for example, he considers as the side farthest from him the outstanding line of an advancing wave, as this line approaches him and rises it hides from his eyes everything behind it; and thus the space under examination is overturned and at the same time crushed.

In any case Mr Palomar does not lose heart and at each moment he thinks he has managed to see everything to be seen from his observation-point, but then something always crops up that he had not borne in mind. If it were not for his impatience to reach a complete, definitive conclusion of his visual operation, looking at waves would be a very restful exercise for him and could save him from neurasthenia, heart attack, and gastric ulcer. And it could perhaps be the key to mastering the world's complexity by reducing it to the simplest mechanism.

But every attempt to define this model must take into account a long wave that is arriving in a direction perpendicular to the breakers and parallel to the shore, creating the flow of a constant, barely-surfacing crest. The shifts of the waves that ruffle towards the shore do not disturb the steady impulse of this compact crest that slices them at a right angle; and there is no knowing where it comes from or where it then goes. Perhaps it is a breath of east wind that stirs the sea's surface against the deep drive that comes from the mass of water far out at sea, but this wave born of air, in passing, receives also the oblique thrusts from the water's depth and redirects them, straightening them in its own direction and bearing them along. And so the wave continues to grow and gain strength until the clash with contrary waves gradually dulls it and makes it disappear, or else twists it until it is confused in one of the many dynasties of oblique waves slammed, with them, against the shore.

Concentrating the attention on one aspect makes it leap into the foreground and occupy the square, just as, with certain drawings, you have only to close your eyes and when you open them the perspective has changed. Now in the overlapping of crests moving in various directions the general pattern seems broken down into sections that rise and vanish. In addition, the reflux of every wave also has a power of its own that hinders the oncoming waves. And if you concentrate your attention on these backward thrusts it seems that the true movement is the one that begins from the shore and goes out to sea.

Is this perhaps the real result that Mr Palomar is about to achieve? To make the waves run in the opposite direction, to overturn time, to perceive the true substance of the world beyond sensory and mental habits? No, he feels a slight dizziness, but it goes no farther than that. The stubbornness that drives the waves towards the shore wins the match: in fact, the waves have swelled considerably. Is the wind about to change? It would be disastrous if the image that Mr Palomar has succeeded painstakingly in putting together were to shatter and be lost. Only if he manages to bear all the aspects in mind at once can he begin the second phase of the operation: extending this knowledge to the entire universe.

It would suffice not to lose patience, as he soon does. Mr Palomar goes off along the beach, tense and nervous as when he came, and even more unsure about everything.

The naked bosom

Mr Palomar is walking along a lonely beach. He encounters few bathers. One young woman is lying on the sand taking the sun, her bosom bared. Palomar, discreet by nature, looks away at the horizon of the sea. He knows that in such circumstances, at the approach of a strange man, women often cover themselves hastily, and this does not seem right to him: because it is a nuisance for the woman peacefully sun-bathing, and because the passing man feels he is an intruder, and because the taboo against nudity is implicitly confirmed; because half-respected conventions spread insecurity and incoherence of behavior rather than freedom and frankness.

And so, as soon as he sees in the distance the outline of the bronze-pink cloud of a naked female torso, he quickly turns his head in such a way that the trajectory of his gaze remains suspended in the void and guarantees his civil respect for the invisible frontier that surrounds people.

But – he thinks as he proceeds and resumes, the moment the horizon is clear, the free movement of his eyeballs – in acting like this, I display a refusal to see; or, in other words, I am finally reinforcing the convention that declares illicit any sight of the breast; that is to say, I create a kind of mental brassière suspended between my eyes and that bosom that, from the flash that reached the edge of my visual field, seemed to me fresh and pleasant to the eye. In other words, my not looking presupposes that I am thinking of that nakedness, worrying about it; and this is basically an indiscreet and reactionary attitude.

Returning from his stroll, Palomar again passes that bather, and this time he keeps his eyes fixed straight ahead, so that his gaze touches with impartial uniformity the foam of the retreating waves, the boats pulled up on shore, the great bath-towel spread out on the sand, the swelling moon of lighter skin with the dark halo of the nipple, the outline of the coast in the haze, gray against the sky.

There – he reflects, pleased with himself, as he continues on his way – I have succeeded in having the bosom completely absorbed by the landscape, so that my gaze counted no more than the gaze of a seagull or a hake.

But is this really the right way to act, he reflects further. Or does it not mean flattening the human person to the level of things, considering it an object, and, worse still, considering as object that which in the person is the specific attribute of the female sex? Am I not perhaps perpetuating the old habit of male superiority, hardened over the years into a habitual insolence?

He turns and retraces his steps. Now, in allowing his gaze to run over the beach with neutral objectivity, he arranges it so that, once the woman's bosom enters his field of vision, a break is noticeable, a shift, almost a darting glance. That glance goes on to graze the taut skin, withdraws, as if appreciating with a slight start the different consistency of the view and the special value it acquires, and for a moment the glance hovers in mid-air, making a curve that accompanies the swell of the breast from a certain distance, elusively but also protectively, to then continue its course as if nothing had happened.

In this way I believe my position is made quite clear, Palomar thinks, with no possible misunderstandings. But couldn't this grazing of his eyes be finally taken for an attitude of superiority, an underestimation of what a breast is and means, a somehow putting it aside, on the margin, or in parenthesis? So, I am relegating the bosom again to the semi-darkness where centuries of sexomaniac puritanism and desire considered as sin have kept it . . .

This interpretation runs counter to Palomar's best intentions, for though he belongs to a human generation for whom nudity of the female bosom was associated with the idea of amorous intimacy, still he hails approvingly this change in customs, both for what it signifies as the reflection of a more broad-minded society and because this sight in particular is pleasing to him. It is this detached encouragement that he would like to be able to express with his gaze.

He does an about-face. With firm steps he walks again towards the woman lying in the sun. Now his gaze, giving the landscape a fickle glance, will linger on the breast with special consideration, but will quickly include it in an impulse of good-will and gratitude for the whole, for the sun and the sky, for the bent pines and the dune and the beach and the rocks and the clouds and the seaweed, for the cosmos that rotates around those haloed cusps.

This should be enough to reassure once and for all the solitary sun-bather and clear away all perverse assumptions. But the moment he approaches again, she suddenly springs up, covers herself with an impatient huff, and goes off, shrugging in irritation, as if she were avoiding the tiresome insistence of a satyr.

The dead weight of an intolerant tradition prevents anyone's understanding, as they deserve, the most enlightened intentions, Palomar bitterly concludes.

The sword of the sun

When the sun begins to go down, its reflection takes form on the sea: from the horizon all the way to the shore a dazzling patch extends composed of countless, swaying glints; between one glint and the next, the opaque blue of the sea makes a dark network. The white boats, seen against the light, turn black, lose substance and bulk, as if they were consumed by that splendid speckling.

This is the hour when Mr Palomar, belated by nature, takes his evening swim. He enters the sea, moves away from the shore, and the sun's reflection becomes a shining sword in the water stretching from the shore to him. Mr Palomar swims in that sword or, more precisely, that sword remains always before him; at every stroke of his, it retreats, and never allows him to overtake it. Wherever he stretches out his arms, the sea takes on its opaque evening color, which extends to the shore behind him.

As the sun sinks towards sunset, the incandescent-white reflection acquires gold and copper tones. And wherever Mr Palomar moves, he remains the vertex of that sharp, gilded triangle; the sword follows him, pointing him out like the hand of a watch whose pivot is the sun.

"This is a special homage the sun pays to me personally," Mr Palomar is tempted to think, or rather the egocentric, megalomaniac ego that dwells in him is tempted to think.

But the depressive and self-wounding ego, who dwells with the other in the same container, rebuts: "Everyone with eyes sees the reflection that follows him; illusion of the senses and of the mind holds us all prisoners always." A third tenant, a more even-handed ego, speaks up: "This means that, no matter what, I am part of the feeling and thinking subjects, capable of establishing a relationship with the sun's rays, and of interpreting and evaluating perceptions and illusions."

Every bather swimming westwards at this hour sees the strip of light aimed at him, which then dies out just a bit beyond the spot where his arm extends: each has his *own* reflection, which has that direction only for him and moves with him. On either side of the reflection, the water's blue is darker. "Is that the only non-illusory datum, common to all: darkness?" Mr Palomar wonders. But the sword is imposed equally on the eye of each swimmer; there is no avoiding it. "Is what we have in common precisely what is given to each of us as something exclusively his?"

The sailboards slide over the water, cutting with sidelong swerves the land wind that springs up at this hour. Erect figures hold the boom with arms extended like archers', competing for the air that snaps the canvas. When they cross the reflection, in the midst of the gold that enshrouds them the colors of the sails are muted and the outline of opaque bodies seems to enter the night.

"All this is happening not on the sea, not in the sun," the swimmer Palomar thinks, "but inside my head, in the circuits between eyes and brain. I am swimming in my mind; this sword of light exists only there; and this is precisely what attracts me. This is my element, the only one I can know in some way."

But he also thinks: "I cannot reach it: it is always there ahead, it cannot be at once inside me and something inside which I am swimming; if I see it I remain outside it, and it remains outside."

His strokes have become weary and hesitant; you would

think that all his reasoning, rather than increase his pleasure in swimming in the reflection, is spoiling it for him, making him feel it as a limitation, or a guilt, or a condemnation. And also a responsibility he cannot escape: the sword exists only because he is there; and if he were to go away, if all the swimmers and craft were to return to the shore, or simply turn their backs on the sun, where would the sword end? In the disintegrating world the thing he would like to save is the most fragile: that sea-bridge between his eyes and the sinking sun. Mr Palomar no longer feels like swimming; he is cold. But he goes on: now he is obliged to stay in the water until the sun has disappeared.

Then he thinks: "If I see and think and swim the reflection, it is because at the other extreme there is the sun that casts its rays. Only the origin of what is matters: something that my gaze cannot face except in an attenuated form, as in this sunset. All the rest is reflection among reflections, me included."

The ghost of a sail passes; the shadow of the man-mast flows among the luminous scales. "Without the wind this trap put together with plastic joints, human bones and tendons, nylon sheets, would not stand up; it is the wind that makes it a craft that seems endowed with an end and a purpose of its own; it is only the wind that knows where the surf and the surfer are heading," he thinks. What a relief it would be if he could manage to cancel his partial and doubting ego in the certitude of a principle from which everything is derived! A single, absolute principle from which actions and forms are derived? Or else a certain number of distinct principles, lines of force that intersect, giving a form to the world as it appears, unique, instant by instant?

". . . the wind and, obviously, the sea, the mass of water that supports the floating and shifting solid bodies, like me and the sailboard," Palomar thinks, in a dead-man's float.

His upside-down gaze now contemplates the straying clouds and the hills clouded with woods. His ego is also turned upside down in the elements: the celestial fire, the racing air, the water-cradle and the earth-support. Can this be nature? But nothing of what he sees exists in nature: the sun does not set, the sea does not have this color, the shapes are not those that the light casts on his retina. With unnatural movements of his limbs, he is floating among phantoms; human forms in unnatural positions, shifting their weight to exploit not the wind but the geometrical abstraction of an angle made by wind and the tilting of an artificial device, and thus they glide over the smooth skin of the sea. Does nature not exist?

The swimming ego of Mr Palomar is immersed in a disembodied world, intersections of fields of force, vectorial diagrams, bands of position lines that converge, diverge, break up. But inside him there remains one point in which everything exists in another way, like a lump, like a clot, like a blockage: the sensation that you are here but could not be here, in a world that could not be, but is.

An intrusive wave troubles the smooth sea; a motorboat bursts forth and speeds off, spilling fuel and skipping on its flat belly. In greasy, multicolored glints the skin of oil spreads out, rippling in the water; that material consistency lacking in the glint of the sun cannot be doubted thanks to this trace of the physical presence of man, who scatters excess fuel in his wake, detritus of combustion, residues that cannot be assimilated, mixing and multiplying the life and death around him.

"This is my habitat," Palomar thinks, "which it is not a question of accepting or rejecting, because I can exist only here, within it." But if the fate of life on earth were already sealed? If the race towards death were to become stronger than any possibility of rescue?

The wave flows, a solitary breaker, until it crashes on the shore; and where there seemed to be only sand, gravel, seaweeds and minute shells, the withdrawal of the water now reveals a margin of beach dotted with cans, peanuts, condoms, dead fish, plastic bottles, broken clogs, syringes, twigs black with oil.

Lifted also by the motorboat's wave, swept off by the tide of residue, Mr Palomar suddenly feels like flotsam amid flotsam, a corpse rolling on the garbage-beaches of the cemetery-continents. If no eye except the glassy eye of the dead were to open again on the surface of the terraqueous globe, the sword would not gleam any more.

When you come to think about it, such a situation is not new: for millions of centuries the sun's rays rested on the water before there were eyes capable of perceiving them.

Mr Palomar swims under water, surfaces; there is the sword! One day an eye emerged from the sea, and the sword, already there waiting for it, could finally display its fine, sharp tip and its gleaming splendor. They were made for each other, sword and eye: and perhaps it was not the birth of the eye that caused the birth of the sword, but vice versa, because the sword had to have an eye to observe it at its climax.

Mr Palomar thinks of the world without him: that endless world before his birth, and that far more obscure world after his death; he tries to imagine the world before eyes, any eyes; and a world that tomorrow, through catastrophe or slow corrosion, will be left blind. What happens (happened, will happen) in that world? Promptly an arrow of light sets out from the sun, is reflected in the calm sea, sparkles in the tremolo of the water; and then matter becomes receptive to light, is differentiated into living tissues, and all of a sudden an eye, a multitude of eyes, burgeons, or reburgeons . . .

Now all the sailboards have been pulled ashore, and the last shivering swimmer – Palomar by name – also comes out of the water. He has become convinced that the sword will exist even without him: finally he dries himself with a soft towel and goes home.

PALOMAR IN THE GARDEN

The loves of the tortoises

There are two tortoises on the patio: a male and a female. Zlak! Zlak! their shells strike each other. It is the season of their love-making.

The male pushes the female sideways, all around the edge of the paving. The female seems to resist his attack, or at least she opposes a somewhat inert immobility. The male is smaller and more active; he seems younger. He tries repeatedly to mount her, from behind, but the back of her shell is steep and he slides off.

Now he must have succeeded in achieving the right position: he thrusts with rhythmic, cadenced strokes; at every thrust he emits a kind of gasp, almost a cry. The female has her foreclaws flattened against the ground, enabling her to raise her hind part. The male scratches with his foreclaws on her shell, his neck stuck out, his mouth gaping. The problem with these shells is that there's no way to get a hold; and, in fact, the claws can find no purchase.

Now she escapes him, he pursues her. Not that she is faster or particularly determined to run away: to restrain her he gives her some little nips on one leg, always the same one. She does not rebel. Every time she stops, the male tries to mount her; but she takes a little step forward and he topples off, slamming his member on the ground. This member is fairly long, hooked in a way that apparently makes it possible for him to reach her even though the thickness of the shells and their awkward positioning separates them. So there is no telling how many of these attacks achieve their purpose or how many fail, or how many are theater, play-acting.

It is summer; the patio is bare, except for one green jasmine in a corner. The courtship consists of making so many turns around the little patch of grass, with pursuits and flights and skirmishing not of the claws but of the shells, which strike in a dull clicking. The female tries to find refuge among the stalks of the jasmine; she believes – or wants to make others believe – that she does this to hide; but actually this is the surest way to remain blocked by the male, held immobile with no avenue of escape. Now it is likely that he has managed to introduce his member properly; but this time they are both completely still, silent.

The sensations of the pair of mating tortoises are something Mr Palomar cannot imagine. He observes them with a cold attention, as if they were two machines: two electronic tortoises programmed to mate. What does eros become if there are plates of bone or horny scales in the place of skin? But what we call eros – is it perhaps only a program of our corporeal bodies, more complicated because the memory receives messages from every cell of the skin, from every molecule of our tissues, and multiplies them and combines them with the impulses transmitted by our eyesight and with those aroused by the imagination? The difference lies only in the number of circuits involved: from our receptors billions of wires extend, linked with the computer of feelings, conditionings, the ties between one person and another . . . Eros is a program that unfolds in the electronic clusters of the mind, but the mind is also skin: skin touched, seen, remembered. And what about the tortoises, enclosed in their insensitive casing? The poverty of their sensorial stimuli perhaps drives them to a concentrated, intense mental life, leads them to a crystalline inner awareness . . . Perhaps the eros of tortoises obeys absolute spiritual laws, while we are prisoners of a machinery whose functioning remains unknown to us, prone to clogging up, stalling, exploding in uncontrolled automatisms . . .

Do the tortoises understand themselves any better? After about ten minutes of mating, the two shells separate. She ahead, he behind, they resume their circling of the grass. Now the male remains more distanced, every now and then he scratches his claws against her shell, he climbs on her for a little, but without much conviction. They go back under the jasmine. He gives her a nip or two on one leg, always in the same place.

The blackbird's whistle

Mr Palomar is lucky in one respect: he spends the summer in a place where many birds sing. As he sits in a deck-chair and "works" (in fact, he is lucky also in another respect: he can say he is working in places and attitudes that would suggest complete repose; or rather, he suffers this handicap: he feels obliged never to stop working, even when lying under the trees on an August morning), the invisible birds among the boughs around him display a repertory of the most varied manifestations of sound; they enfold him in an acoustic space that is irregular, discontinuous, jagged; but thanks to an equilibrium established among the various sounds, none of which outdoes the others in intensity or frequency, all is woven into a homogeneous texture, held together not by harmony but by lightness and transparency. Until the hour of greatest heat, when the fierce horde of insects asserts its absolute domination of the vibrations of the air, systematically filling the dimensions of time and space with the deafening and ceaseless hammering of cicadas.

The birds' song occupies a variable part of Mr Palomar's auditory attention: at times he ignores it as a component of the basic silence, at other times he concentrates on distinguishing, within it, one song from another, grouping them into categories of increasing complexity: punctiform chirps; two-note trills (one note long, one short); brief, vibrato whistling; gurgles, little cascades of notes that pour down, spin out, then stop; twirls of modulation that twist upon themselves, and so on, to extended warbling.

Mr Palomar does not arrive at a less generic classification: he is not one of those people who, on hearing a bird-call, can identify the bird it belongs to. This ignorance makes him feel guilty. The new knowledge the human race is acquiring does not compensate for the knowledge spread only by direct oral transmission, which, once lost, cannot be regained or retransmitted: no book can teach what can be learned only in childhood if you lend an alert ear and eye to the song and flight of birds and if you find someone who knows how to give them a specific name. Rather than the cultivation of precise nomenclature and classification, Palomar had preferred the constant pursuit of a precision unsure in defining the modulating, the shifting, the composite. Today he would make the opposite choice, and following the train of thoughts stirred by the birds' singing, he sees his life as a series of missed opportunities.

Among all the cries of the birds, the blackbird's whistle stands out, unmistakable for any other. The blackbirds arrive in the late afternoon; there are two of them, a couple certainly, perhaps the same couple as last year, as every year at this season. Each afternoon, hearing a whistled summons, on two notes, like the signal of a person wishing to announce his arrival, Mr Palomar raises his head to look around for whoever is calling him. Then he remembers that this is the blackbirds' hour. He soon glimpses them: they walk on the lawn as if their true vocation were to be earth-bound bipeds, and as if they enjoyed establishing analogies with human beings.

The blackbird's whistle has this special quality: it is identical with a human whistle, the effort of someone not terribly skilled at whistling, but with a good reason for whistling, this once, only this once, with no intention of continuing, a person who does it with a determined, but modest and affable tone, calculated to win the indulgence of anyone who hears him.

After a while the whistle is repeated – by the same black-bird or by its mate – but always as if this were the first time it had occurred to him to whistle; if this is a dialogue, each remark is uttered after long reflection. But is it a dialogue, or does each blackbird whistle for itself and not for the other? And, in whichever case, are these questions and answers (to the whistler or to the mate) or are they confirmations of something that is always the same thing (the bird's own presence, his belonging to this species, this sex, this terri-tory)? Perhaps the value of this single word lies in its being repeated by another whistling beak, in its not being forgotten during the interval of silence.

Or else the whole dialogue consists of one saying to the other "I am here," and the length of the pauses adds to the phrase the sense of a "still," as if to say: "I am here still, it is still I." And what if it is in the pause and not in the whistle that the meaning of the message is contained? If it were in the silence that the blackbirds speak to each other? (In this case the whistle would be a punctuation mark, a formula like "over and out.") A silence, apparently the same as another silence, could express a hundred different notions; a whistle could too, for that matter; to speak to one another by remaining silent, or by whistling, is always possible; the problem is understanding one another. Or perhaps no one can understand anyone: each blackbird believes that he has put into his whistle a meaning fundamental for him, but only he understands it; the other gives him a reply that has no connection with what he said; it is a dialogue between the deaf, a conversation without head or tail.

But is human dialogue really any different? Mrs Palomar is also in the garden, watering the veronicas. She says, "There they are," a pleonastic utterance (if it assumes that her husband is already looking at the blackbirds), or else (if he has not seen them) incomprehensible, but in any event intended to establish her own priority in the observation of the blackbirds (because, in fact, she was the first to discover them and to point out their habits to her husband) and to underline their unfailing appearance, which she has already reported many times.

"Sssh," Mr Palomar says, apparently to prevent his wife from frightening them by speaking in a loud voice (useless injunction because the blackbirds, husband and wife, are by now accustomed to the presence and voices of Palomars, husband and wife) but actually to contest the wife's precedence, displaying a consideration for the blackbirds far greater than hers.

Then Mrs Palomar says, "It's dry again, just since yesterday," meaning the earth in the flowerbed she is watering, a communication in itself superfluous, but meant to show, as she continues speaking and changes the subject, a far greater familiarity and nonchalance with the blackbirds than her husband has. In any case, from these remarks Mr Palomar derives a general picture of tranquility, and he is grateful to his wife for it, because if she confirms the fact that for the moment there is nothing more serious for him to bother about, then he can remain absorbed in his work (or pseudo-work or hyperwork). He allows a minute to pass, then he also tries to send a reassuring message, to inform his wife that his work (or infrawork or ultrawork) is proceeding as usual: to this end he emits a series of sighs and grumbles: "crooked . . . for all that . . . repeat . . . yes, my foot . . .": utterances that, taken all together, transmit also the message "I am very busy," in the event that his wife's last remark contained a veiled reproach on the order of "you could also assume some responsibility for watering the garden."

The premiss of these verbal exchanges is the idea that a perfect accord between a married pair allows them to understand each other without having to make everything specific and detailed; but this principle is put into practice in very different ways by the two of them: Mrs Palomar expresses herself with complete sentences, though often allusive or sibylline, to test the promptness of her husband's mental associations and the syntony of his thoughts with hers (a thing that does not always work); Mr Palomar, on the other hand, from the mists of his inner monologue allows scattered, articulate sounds to emerge, confident that, if the obviousness of a complete meaning does not emerge, at least the chiaroscuro of a mood will.

Mrs Palomar, instead, refuses to receive these grumbles as talk, and to underline her non-participation she says in a low voice, "Sssh! . . . You'll frighten them . . .", applying to her husband the same shushing that he had believed himself entitled to impose on her, and confirming once more her own primacy as far as consideration for the blackbirds goes.

Having scored this point to her advantage, Mrs Palomar goes off. The blackbirds peck on the lawn and no doubt consider the dialogue of the Palomars the equivalent of their own whistles. We might just as well confine ourselves to whistling, he thinks. Here a prospect that is very promising for Mr Palomar's thinking opens out; for him the discrepancy between human behavior and the rest of the universe has always been a source of anguish. The equal whistle of man and blackbird now seems to him a bridge thrown over the abyss.

If man were to invest in whistling everything he normally entrusts to words, and if the blackbird were to modulate into his whistling all the unspoken truth of his natural condition, then the first step would be taken towards bridging the gap between . . . between what and what? Nature and culture? Silence and speech? Mr Palomar hopes always that silence contains something more than what language can say. But what if language were really the goal towards which every-thing in existence tends? Or what if everything that exists were language, and has been since the beginning of time? Here Mr Palomar is again gripped by anguish.

After having listened carefully to the whistle of the black-bird, he tries to repeat it, as faithfully as he can. A puzzled silence follows, as if his message required careful examination; then an identical whistle re-echoes. Mr Palomar does not know if this is a reply to his, or the proof that his whistle is so different that the blackbirds are not the least disturbed by it and resume their dialogue as if nothing had happened.

They go on whistling, questioning in their puzzlement, he and the blackbirds.

The infinite lawn

Around Mr Palomar's house there is a lawn. This is not a place where a lawn should exist naturally: so the lawn is an artificial object, composed from natural objects, namely grasses. The lawn's purpose is to represent nature, and this representation occurs as the substitution of the nature proper to the area with a nature in itself natural but artificial for this area. In other words, it costs money: the lawn requires expense and endless labor to sow it, water it, fertilize it, weed it, mow it.

The lawn is composed of dicondra, darnel and clover. This mixture, in equal parts, was scattered over the ground at sowing time. The dicondra, dwarfed and creeping, promptly got the upper hand: its carpet of soft little round leaves spreads everywhere, pleasing to the foot and to the eye. But the lawn is given its thickness by the sharp spears of darnel, if they are not too sparse and if you do not allow them to grow too much before cutting them. The clover sprouts irregularly, some clumps here, nothing there, and farther on, a whole sea of it; it grows exuberantly until it slumps, because the helix of the leaf becomes top-heavy and bends the tender stalk. The lawn-mower attends with deafening shudder to the tonsure; a light odor of fresh hay intoxicates the air; the leveled grass finds again a bristling infancy, but the bite of the blades reveals unevenness, mangy clearings, yellow patches.

To cut its proper figure, the lawn must be a uniform green expanse: an unnatural result that lawns created by nature achieve naturally. Here, observing it point by point, you discover where the whirling jet of the hose cannot reach, and where the water falls constantly and rots the roots, and where the carefully-regulated watering fosters weeds.

Mr Palomar is crouched on the lawn, pulling up weeds. A dandelion clings to the ground with a foundation of jagged leaves, thickly overlapping; if you tug at the stalk, it breaks off in your hand, while the roots are still sunk into the ground. With a curving movement of the hand you have to grasp the entire plant and delicately slip the roots from the earth, even if you have to pull up a bit of sod and some of the lawn's rare blades of grass, half-smothered by their aggressive neighbor. Then you must throw the interloper in a place where it cannot put down roots again or scatter seed. When you start pulling up one weed, you immediately see another appear a bit farther on, and another, and still another. In no time that stretch of lawn, so grassy that it seemed to need only a few touches, proves to be a lawless jungle.

Are only weeds left? Worse: the harmful grasses are so thickly interwoven with the good that you cannot just thrust in your hand and pull. A complicity seems to have been established between the sown grasses and the wild ones, a relaxing of the barriers imposed by difference of birth, a tolerance resigned to deterioration. Some spontaneous grasses, in and of themselves, do not look at all maleficent or insidious. Why not admit them to the company of those that rightfully belong to the lawn, integrating them in the community of the cultivated plants? This is the road that leads to forgetting about the "English-style lawn" and falling back on the "rustic lawn", left to its own devices. "Sooner or later we'll have to make up our minds and accept it," Mr Palomar thinks, but he feels it would be a betrayal of one's code of honor. A chicory, a borage plant spring into his field of vision. He uproots them.

To be sure, pulling up a weed here and there solves
nothing. This is how it should be done – he thinks: take a
square section of the lawn, one meter by one meter, and
eliminate even the slightest presence of anything but clover,
darnel, or dicondra. Then move on to another square. No,
perhaps not: remain perhaps with a sample square. Count
how many blades of grass there are, what species, how thick,
how distributed. On the basis of this calculation you would
arrive at a statistical knowledge of the lawn, which, once
established . . .

But counting the blades of grass is futile: you would never
learn their number. A lawn does not have precise boundaries,
there is a border where the grass stops growing but still a few
scattered blades sprout farther on, then a thick green clod,
then a sparser stretch: are they still part of the lawn, or not?
Elsewhere the underbrush enters the lawn: you cannot tell
what is lawn and what is bush. But even where there is no
grass, you never know at what point you can stop counting:
between one little plant and the next there is always a tiny
sprouting leaf that barely emerges from the earth, its root a
white wisp hardly perceptible; a moment ago it could have
been overlooked but soon it will also have to be counted.
Meanwhile two other shoots that just now seemed barely
a shade yellowish have definitively withered and must be
erased from the count. Then there are the fractions of blades
of grass, cut in half, or shorn to the ground, or split along the
nervation, the little leaves that have lost one lobe . . . The
decimals, added up, do not make an integer, they remain a
minute grassy devastation, in part still alive, in part already
pulp, food for others plants, humus . . .

The lawn is a collection of grasses – this is how the problem must be formulated – that includes a subcollection of
cultivated grasses and a subcollection of spontaneous grasses
known as weeds; an intersection of the two subcollections
is formed by the grasses which have grown spontaneously
but belong to the cultivated species and are therefore

indistinguishable from them. The two subcollections, in their turn, include various species, each of which is a subcollection, or rather it is a collection that includes the subcollection of its own members, which are members also of the lawn and the subcollection of those alien to the lawn. The wind blows, seeds and pollens fly, the relations among the collections are disrupted . . .

Palomar has already moved to another train of thought: is "the lawn" what we see or do we see one grass plus one grass plus one grass . . . ? What we call "seeing the lawn" is only an effect of our coarse and slapdash senses; a collection exists only because it is formed of discrete elements. There is no point in counting them, the number does not matter; what matters is grasping in one glance the individual little plants, one by one, in their individualities and differences. And not only seeing them: thinking them. Instead of thinking "lawn", to think of that stalk with two clover leaves, that lanceolate, slightly humped leaf, that delicate corymb . . .

Palomar's mind has wandered, he has stopped pulling up weeds; he no longer thinks of the lawn: he thinks of the universe. He is trying to apply to the universe everything he has thought about the lawn. The universe as regular and ordered cosmos or as chaotic proliferation. The universe perhaps finite but countless, unstable within its borders, which discloses other universes within itself. The universe, collection of celestial bodies, nebulas, fine dust, fields of force, intersections of fields, collections of collections . . .

PALOMAR LOOKS AT THE SKY

Moon in the afternoon

Nobody looks at the moon in the afternoon, and this is the moment when it would most require our attention, since its existence is still in doubt. It is a whitish shadow that surfaces from the intense blue of the sky, charged with solar light; who can assure us that, once again, it will succeed in assuming a form and glow? It is so fragile and pale and slender; only on one side does it begin to assume a distinct outline like the arc of a sickle while the rest is all steeped in azure. It is like a transparent wafer, or a half-dissolved pastille; only here the white circle is not dissolving but condensing, collecting itself at the price of gray-bluish patches and shadows that might belong to the moon's geography or might be spillings of the sky that still soak the satellite, porous as a sponge.

In this phase the sky is still something very compact and concrete and you cannot be sure whether it is from its taut, uninterrupted surface that this round and whitish shape is being detached, its consistency only a bit more solid than the clouds', or whether it is a corrosion of the basic tissue, a rift in the dome, a crevice that opens on to the void behind. The uncertainty is heightened by the irregularity of the figure that on one side is taking shape (where the rays of the setting sun arrive) and on the other lingers in a kind of penumbra. And since the border between the two zones is not sharply defined, the effect is not that of a solid seen in perspective but rather one of those little drawings of the moon on calendars, where a white outline stands within a little dark circle. There would be nothing to object to in this, if it were a moon in the first quarter and not a full, or almost full, moon. This, in fact, is what is being revealed, gradually, as its contrast with the sky becomes stronger and its circumference is being more distinctly outlined, with only a few dents on the eastern edge.

It must be said that the sky's blue has veered successively towards periwinkle, towards violet (the sun's rays have become red), then towards ashen and beige, and each time the whiteness of the moon has received an impulse to emerge more firmly, and, inside it, the more luminous part has gained ground until it now covers the whole disk. It is as if the phases that the moon passes through in a month were covered inside this full or gibbous moon, in the hours between its rising and its setting, with the difference that the round form remains more or less in sight. In the midst of the circle the spots are still there, indeed their chiaroscuro becomes more distinct thanks to the luminosity of the rest, but now there is no doubt that it is the moon that bears them like stains or bruises, and they can no longer be taken for transparences of the sky's ground, rips in the cloak of a bodiless ghost-moon.

What remains uncertain, rather, is whether this gain in evidence and (we might as well say it) splendor is due to the slow retreat of the sky, which, as it moves away, sinks deeper and deeper into darkness, or whether, on the contrary, it is the moon that is coming forward, collecting the previously scattered light and depriving the sky of it, concentrating it all in the round mouth of its funnel.

And, especially, these changes must not make us forget that in the meanwhile the satellite has been shifting in the sky, proceeding westwards and upwards. The moon is the most changeable body in the visible universe, and the most regular in its complicated habits: it never fails to show up for an appointment and you can always wait for it at the appointed spot; but if you leave it in one place you always find it next in another, and if you recall its face turned in a certain way, you see it has already changed its pose, a little or a lot. In any case, following it steadily, you do not realize that it is imperceptibly eluding you. Only the clouds intervene to create the illusion of a rapid dash and rapid metamorphoses, or rather, to underline vividly what would otherwise escape the eye.

The cloud dashes. Gray at first, it becomes milky and shiny, the sky behind it has turned black, it is night, the stars are lighted, the moon is a great, dazzling mirror that flies. Who would recognize in this moon the one of a few hours ago? Now it is a lake of shininess, spurting rays all around, brimming in the darkness with a halo of cold silver, and flooding with white light the streets of the night-walkers.

There is no doubt that what is now beginning is a splendid winter night of full moon. At this point, assured that the moon no longer needs him, Mr Palomar goes home.

The eye and the planets

When he learns that this year, for the entire month of April, the three "external" planets, visible to the naked eye (even his, nearsighted and astigmatic) are all three "in opposition" and therefore visible for the whole night, Mr Palomar rushes out on to the terrace.

Because of the full moon the sky is light. Mars, though close to the great lunar mirror flooded with white light, advances imperiously with its stubborn radiance, its thick, concentrated yellow, so different from all the other yellows of the firmament that it has finally been agreed to call it red, and in moments of inspiration really to see it as red.

Moving your gaze down, continuing eastwards an imaginary arc that should link Regulus with Spica (but Spica can hardly be seen), you encounter, quite distinct, Saturn, with its chilly whitish light, and still farther down there is Jupiter, in the moment of its greatest splendor, a vigorous yellow with a hint of green. The stars all around have paled, except Arcturus, which shines with a defiant air, a bit higher to the east.

To enjoy most fully the triple planetary opposition it is necessary to procure a telescope. Mr Palomar, perhaps because he bears the same name as a famous observatory, can boast some friendships among astronomers, and he is allowed to put his nose beside the eyepiece of a 15cm telescope. It is rather small for scientific research; but, compared to his eyeglasses, it makes quite a difference.

For example, in the telescope Mars proves to be a more perplexed planet than it appears to the naked eye: it seems to have many things to communicate and can bring only a small part of them into focus, as in a stammered, coughing speech. A scarlet halo protrudes around the edge; you can try to tuck it in by regulating the screw, to emphasize the crust of ice of the lower pole. Spots appear and vanish on the surface like clouds or rents in clouds; one becomes stabilized in the shape and position of Australia, and Mr Palomar is convinced that the more clearly he sees that Australia the more the lens is focused, but at the same time he realizes that he is losing other shadows of things that he thought he saw or felt obliged to see.

In other words, it seems to him that if Mars is the planet about which, ever since the days of Schiaparelli, so many things have been said, causing alternate illusions and disappointments, this fact coincides with the difficulty of establishing relations with the planet, as with a person of difficult character. (Unless the difficulty of character is all on Mr Palomar's side: he tries in vain to escape subjectivity by taking refuge among the celestial bodies.)

Quite the opposite is the relationship he establishes with Saturn, the most exciting planet to the person viewing it through a telescope: there it is, very sharp, white, the outlines of the sphere and of the ring precise; a faint parallel, a zebra striping marks the sphere; a darker circumference distinguishes the edge of the ring. This telescope hardly picks up any other details and accentuates the geometrical abstraction of the object; the sense of an extreme difference, rather than diminishing, becomes more prominent now than to the naked eye.

The fact that an object so different from all others, a form that achieves the maximum strangeness with the maximum simplicity and regularity and harmony, is rotating in the sky cheers life and thought.

"If the ancients had been able to see it as I see it now," Mr

Palomar thinks, "they would have thought they had pro-
jected their gaze into the heaven of Plato's ideas, or in the
immaterial space of the postulates of Euclid; but instead,
thanks to some misdirection or other, this sight has been
granted to me, who fear it is too beautiful to be true, too grati-
fying to my imaginary universe to belong to the real world.
But perhaps it is this same distrust of our senses that prevents us
from feeling comfortable in the universe. Perhaps the first rule I
must impose on myself is this: stick to what I see."

Now it seems to him that the ring is swaying slightly, or the
planet is, within the ring, and both seem to rotate in place. In
reality it is Mr Palomar's head that is swaying, as he is forced to
twist his neck to fit his gaze into the eyepiece of the telescope;
but he takes care privately not to deny this illusion, which
coincides with his expectation as it does with natural truth.

Saturn really is like this. Since the Voyager 2 expedition
Mr Palomar has read everything written about the rings: they
are made of microscopic particles; they are made of boulders
of ice separated by abysses; the divisions between the rings
are furrows in which the satellites rotate, sweeping away
matter and piling it up at the sides, like sheepdogs circling
around the flock to keep it compact. He followed the discovery of intertwined rings which were then proved to be
simple circles, much more thin; and the discovery of the
opaque streaks arranged like the spokes of a wheel, later
identified as icy clouds. But the new information does not
deny this essential figure, no different from what was first
seen by Gian Domenico Cassini in 1676, when he discovered
the division between the rings that bears his name.

For the occasion a scrupulous person like Mr Palomar
would naturally have consulted encylopedias and manuals.
Now Saturn, an ever-new object, presents itself to his gaze,
renewing the wonder of the first discovery, and prompting
the regret that Galileo with his blurred spyglass was able only
to conceive a confused idea, of triple body or of sphere with
two handles, and when he was coming close to understanding

how it was made, his eyesight failed and everything plunged into darkness.

Staring at a luminous body too long tires the vision: Mr Palomar closes his eyes; he moves on to Jupiter.

In its majestic but not heavy bulk, Jupiter displays two equatorial stripes like a scarf decorated with interwoven embroideries, of a pale bluish-green. Effects of immense atmospheric storms are translated into a calm, orderly pattern, an elaborate composure. But the real pomp of this luxurious planet are its glittering satellites, all four now in sight along an oblique line, like a scepter shining with jewels.

Discovered by Galileo, who named them *Medicea sidera*, "Medici stars", rebaptized a little later with Ovidian names – Io, Europa, Ganymede, Callisto – by a Dutch astronomer, Jupiter's little planets seem to cast a final glow of neoplatonic Renaissance, as if unaware that the impassive order of the celestial spheres had dissolved, because of the work of their discoverer himself.

A dream of classicality enshrouds Jupiter; gazing at it through the telescope, Mr Palomar awaits an Olympian transfiguration. But he is unable to keep the image sharp: he has to lower his eyelids for a moment, let the dazzled pupil find again the precise perception of outlines, colors, shadows, but also let the imagination strip away borrowed garments and renounce its show of bookish learning.

While it is right for the imagination to come to support weakness of vision, it must be immediate and direct like the gaze that kindles it. What was the first simile that occurred to him and that he dismissed because it was incongruous? He had seen the planet sway with its satellites in line like air-bubbles rising from the gills of a round fish of the depths, luminescent and striped . . .

The following night Mr Palomar goes out on his terrace again, to see the planets with his naked eye: the great difference is that here he is forced to bear in mind the proportions between the planet, the rest of the firmament scattered in dark space on all sides, and himself, watching: something that does not happen if the relation is between the isolated object-planet focused by the lens and himself-subject, in an illusory face-to-face encounter. At the same time he remembers that detailed image of each planet seen last night, and tries to insert it into that minuscule dot of light that pierces the sky. In this way he hopes that he has truly taken possession of the planet, or at least of as much of a planet as can enter inside an eye.

The contemplation of the stars

When it is a beautiful starry night Mr Palomar says: "I *must* go and look at the stars." That is exactly what he says: "I *must*," because he hates waste and believes it is wrong to waste that great quantity of stars that is put at his disposal. He says "I must" also because he has little practical knowledge of how you look at the stars, and this simple action always costs him a certain effort.

The first problem is to find a place from which his gaze can move freely over the whole dome of the sky without obstacles and without the invasion of electric light: for example a lonely beach on a very low coast.

Another necessary condition is to bring along an astronomical chart, without which he would not know what he is looking at; but between times he forgets how to orient it and he has first to devote a half-hour to studying it. To decipher the chart in the darkness he must also bring along a flashlight. The frequent checking of sky against chart requires him to turn the light on and off, and in the passages from light to darkness he remains almost blinded and has to readjust his vision every time.

If Mr Palomar employed a telescope things would be more complicated in some ways and simplified in others; but, for the present, the experience of the sky that interests him is that of the naked eye, like that of ancient navigators and nomad shepherds. Naked eye for him, who is nearsighted, means eyeglasses; and since he has to remove his eyeglasses to study the chart, operations are complicated with this pushing up and lowering of the eyeglasses on his brow and there is a wait of several seconds before his crystalline lenses can focus the real stars or the printed ones. On the chart the names of the stars are written in black on a blue ground, and he has to hold the flashlight against the paper in order to make them out. When he raises his eyes to the sky, he sees it black, scattered with vague glows; only gradually do the stars become fixed, set in precise patterns, and the more he looks, the more stars he sees emerge.

Furthermore the celestial charts he has to consult are two, or rather four: one, very synthetic, of the sky in that month, which presents separately the southern hemisphere and the northern; and one of the entire firmament, much more detailed, which shows in a long strip the constellations of the whole year for the central part of the sky around the horizon, whereas those of the segment around the Pole Star are included in a separate circular map. In other words, to locate a star involves the checking of various maps against the vault of the sky, with all the related actions: putting on and taking off eyeglasses, turning the flashlight on and off, unfolding and folding the large chart, losing and finding again the reference points.

Since the last time Mr Palomar looked at the stars weeks or months have gone by; the sky is all changed. The Great Bear (it is August) is stretched out, almost lying down, on the crowns of the trees to the north-west; Arcturus plunges towards the outline of the hill, dragging all the kite of the Dipper with him; exactly west is Vega, high and solitary; that star over the sea is Altair and up above is Deneb, which emits a cold ray from its zenith.

Tonight the sky seems far more crowded than any chart; the schematic patterns prove in reality to be more complicated and less distinct; each cluster could contain that triangle or that broken line you are seeking; and each time you look up at a constellation it seems a bit different to you.

In identifying a constellation the decisive proof is to see how it answers when you call it. More convincing than the matching of distances and configurations with those marked on the chart is the reply that the luminous dot gives to the name by which it has been called, its promptness in responding to that sound, becoming one with it. For those of us who are ignorant of all mythology, the names of the stars seem incongruous, arbitrary; and yet you could never consider them interchangeable. When the name that Mr Palomar has found is the right one, he realizes it at once, because it gives the star a necessity and an evidence it did not have before; but, on the other hand, if the name is wrong, the star loses it after a few seconds, as if shrugging it off, and you no longer know where it was and who it was.

Several times Mr Palomar decides that the Berenice's Hair (a constellation he loves) is this or that luminous swarm in the direction of Serpentarius: but he does not feel again the throb he felt on previous occasions on recognizing that object, so sumptuous and yet so light. Only later does he realize that he cannot find it because in this season Berenice's Hair cannot be seen.

To a large extent the sky is streaked with light stripes and patches; in August the Milky Way assumes a dense consistency and you would say it is overflowing its bed; the dark and the light are so mixed that they prevent the effect of perspective of a black abyss against whose empty remoteness the stars stand out, in relief; everything remains on the same plane: glitter and silvery cloud and shadows.

Is this the exact geometry of the sidereal spaces, which Mr Palomar has so often felt the need to turn to, in order to detach himself from the Earth, that place of superfluous complications and confused approximations? When he finds himself really in the presence of the starred sky, everything seems to escape him. Even that aspect to which he thought himself most sensitive, the smallness of our world compared to the vast distances, does not emerge directly. The firmament is something that is up there, you can see that it exists, but from it you can derive no idea of dimensions or distance.

If the luminous bodies are filled with uncertainty, the only solution is to entrust oneself to the darkness, to the deserted regions of the sky. What can be more stable than nothingness? And yet we cannot be one hundred per cent sure even of nothingness. Where Palomar sees a clearing in the firmament, a breach, empty and black, he fixes his gaze there, as if projecting himself into it; and then, even there, some brighter grain begins to form, a little patch or dot; but he cannot be sure if they are really there or if he just seems to see them. Perhaps it is a glow like those you see rotating when you keep your eyes shut (the dark sky is like the obverse of the eyelids, furrowed by phosphenes); perhaps it is a glint from his eyeglasses; but it could also be an unknown star surfacing from the most remote depths.

This observation of the stars transmits an unstable and contradictory knowledge – Palomar thinks – the exact opposite of what the ancients were able to derive from it. Is this because his relationship with the sky is intermittent and agitated rather than a serene habit? If he forced himself to contemplate the constellations night after night and year after year, following their progress, their returns along the curved tracks of the dark vault, he would perhaps also gain in the end the notion of a continuing and unchangeable time, separated from the labile and fragmentary time of terrestrial events. But would attention to the celestial revolutions be enough to stamp this imprint on him? Or would not a special inner revolution be necessary, something he could suppose only theoretically, unable to imagine the palpable effects on his emotions and on the rhythms of his mind?

Of the mythical knowledge of the stars he picks up only a weary glimmering; of the scientific knowledge, the echoes popularized by the newspapers. He distrusts what he knows;

what he does not know keeps his spirit in a suspended state. Oppressed, insecure, he becomes nervous over the celestial charts as over the railroad timetables when he flips through them in search of a connection.

There, a glowing arrow slices the sky. A meteor? These are the nights when you sight shooting stars most frequently. But it could also easily be a brightly-lighted commercial plane. Mr Palomar's gaze remains alert, available, released from all certitude.

He has been on the dark beach for an hour, seated on a deck-chair, twisting towards south or towards north, every now and then turning on the flashlight and holding the charts to his nose, after keeping them spread out on his lap; then, craning his neck backwards he begins the exploration again, setting out from the Pole Star.

Some silent shadows are moving over the sand: a pair of lovers rises from the dune, a night fisherman, a customs-man, a boatman. Mr Palomar hears a whispering. He looks around: a few paces from him a little crowd has gathered, observing his movements like the convulsions of a madman.

PALOMAR IN THE CITY

PALOMAR ON THE TERRACE

From the terrace

"Shoo! Shoo!" Mr Palomar rushes on to the terrace to drive away the pigeons, who eat the leaves of the gazania, riddle the succulent plants with their beaks, cling with their claws to the cascade of morning-glories, peck at the blackberries, devour leaf by leaf the parsley planted in the box near the kitchen, dig and scratch in the flowerpots, spilling dirt and baring the roots, as if the sole purpose of their flights were devastation. The doves whose flying once cheered the city's squares have been followed by a degenerate progeny, filthy and infected, neither domestic nor wild, but integrated into the public institutions and, as such, inextinguishable. The sky of Rome has long since fallen under the dominion of the over-population of these lumpen-fowl, who make life difficult for every other species of bird in the area and oppress the once free and various kingdom of the air with their monotonous, moulting, lead-gray livery.

Trapped between the subterranean hordes of rats and the grievous flight of the pigeons, the ancient city allows itself to be corroded from below and from above, offering no more resistance than it did in the past to the barbarian invasions, as if it saw not the assault of external enemies but the darkest, most congenital impulses of its own inner essence.

The city has also another soul – one of the many – that lives on the harmony between old stones and ever-new

vegetation, sharing the favors of the sun. Fostering this good
environmental attitude or *genius loci*, the Palomar family's
terrace, a secret island above the rooftops, dreams of concentrating under its pergola the luxuriance of the gardens of
Babylon.

The luxuriance of the terrace corresponds to the desire of
each member of the family. For Mrs Palomar it was natural
to transfer to the plants her attention to individual things,
chosen and made her own through an inner identification and
thus becoming part of a composition with multiple variations, an emblematic collection; but this spiritual dimension
is lacking in the other members of the family. In the daughter
because youth cannot and should not become fixed on the
here but only on the farther on, the over there; in the husband
because he was too late in freeing himself from his youthful
impatiences and in understanding (only in theory) that salva-
tion lies solely in applying oneself to the things that there are.

The concerns of the cultivator, for whom what matters
is that given plant, that given piece of ground exposed to
the sun from this hour to that hour, that given disease of
the leaves which must be fought in time with that given
treatment, are alien to the mind modeled on the processes
of industry, led to make decisions, in other words, along
general lines, according to prototypes. When Palomar realized
how approximate and doomed to error are the criteria of that
world, where he had thought to find precision and universal
norms, he slowly reverted to building for himself a relationship with the world, confining it to the observation of
visible forms; but by then he was the way he was: his connection with things has remained that intermittent and labile
tie of those people who seem always intent on thinking
of something else, but this something else does not exist.
His contribution to the burgeoning of the terrace is to run
out every now and then to frighten the pigeons — "Shoo!
Shoo!" — waking in himself the atavistic sense of defending
the territory.

If birds other than pigeons light on the terrace, instead of driving them away Mr Palomar welcomes them, closes an eye to any possible damage done by their beaks, considers them the messengers of friendly deities. But these appearances are rare: a patrol of crows occasionally approaches, punctuating the sky with black patches, and spreading (even the language of the gods changes with the centuries) a sense of life and gaiety. Then an occasional blackbird, polite and clever; once, a robin; sparrows in their usual role of anonymous passers-by. Other feathered presences over the city allow themselves to be sighted at a greater distance: the squadrons of migratory birds, in autumn, and the acrobatics, in summer, of swallows and house martins. From time to time, white gulls, rowing the air with their long wings, venture over the dry sea of tiles, lost perhaps in following the bends of the river from its mouth, or perhaps intent on a nuptial rite, and their marine cry shrieks among the city noises.

The terrace is on two levels: a loggia or belvedere dominates the hurly-burly of the roofs over which Mr Palomar casts a bird's-eye glance. He tries to conceive the world as it is seen by birds; unlike him, birds have the void opening beneath them, but perhaps they never look down, they see only to the side, hovering obliquely on their wings, and their gaze, like his, wherever it turns, encounters nothing but roofs, higher or lower, constructions more or less elevated but so thick that he can move but so far down. That down below, hemmed in, streets and squares exist, that the true ground is the one at ground level, he knows on the basis of other experiences; at this moment, from what he can see from up here, he would never suspect it.

The true form of the city is in this rise and fall of roofs, old tiles and new, curved and flat, slender or squat chimneys, arbors of reed matting and sheds of corrugated iron, railings, balustrades, little columns supporting pots, metal water-tanks, dormers, glass skylights, and rising above all else the

rigging of TV aerials, straight or crooked, enameled or rust-
ing, in models of successive generations, variously ramified
and horned and shielded, but all of them thin as skeletons and
disturbing as totems. Separated by irregular and jagged gulfs
of emptiness, proletarian terraces with lines for drying laun-
dry and with tomato plants growing in tin cans directly face
residential terraces with espaliered plants growing against
wooden trellises, garden furniture of white-painted cast iron,
awnings; and campaniles with the bell-chamber pealing;
façades of public buildings, in profile and full-face; garrets
and penthouses, illegal and unpunished constructions; pipe-
scaffoldings of constructions in progress or left half-finished;
large windows with curtains and little WC windows; ochre
walls and burnt sienna walls, walls the color of mold from
whose crevices clumps of weeds spill their pendulous foliage;
elevator shafts; towers with double and triple mullioned
windows; spires of churches with madonnas; statues of
horses and chariots; great mansions which have decayed
into hovels, hovels restructured into smart bachelor apart-
ments; and domes that make round outlines against the sky in
every direction and at every distance as if to confirm the
female, Junoesque essence of the city: white domes or pink or
violet according to the hour and the light, veined with nerva-
tures, crowned by lanterns surmounted by other, smaller
domes.

Nothing of this can be seen by one who moves on his
feet or his wheels over the city pavements. And, inversely,
from up here you have the impression that the true crust
of the earth is this, uneven but compact, even if furrowed
by gaps whose depth cannot be known, chasms or pits or
craters, whose edges seem in perspective to overlap like the
scales of a pine cone, and it never even occurs to you to
wonder what is hidden in their depth, because the panorama
of the surface is already so vast and rich and various that it
more than suffices to saturate the mind with information and
meanings.

This is how birds think, or at least this is how Mr Palomar thinks, imagining himself a bird. "It is only after you have come to know the surface of things," he concludes, "that you venture to seek what is underneath. But the surface is inexhaustible."

The gecko's belly

On the terrace, the gecko has returned, as he does every summer. An exceptional observation point allows Mr Palomar to see him not from above, as we have always been accustomed to seeing geckos, treefrogs, and lizards, but from below. In the living room of the Palomar home there is a little show-case window and display case that opens on to the terrace; on the shelves of this case a collection of Art Nouveau vases is aligned; in the evening a 75-Watt bulb illuminates the objects; a plumbago plant trails its pale blue flowers from the wall against the outside glass; every evening, as soon as the light is turned on, the gecko, who lives under the leaves on that wall, moves onto the glass, to the spot where the bulb shines, and remains motionless, like a lizard in the sun. Gnats fly around, also attracted by the light; the reptile, when a gnat comes within range, swallows it.

Mr Palomar and Mrs Palomar every evening end up shifting their chairs from the television set to place them near the glass; from the interior of the room they contemplate the whitish form of the reptile against the dark background. The choice between television and gecko is not always made without some hesitation; each of the two spectacles has some information to offer that the other does not provide: the television ranges over continents gathering luminous impulses that describe the visible face of things; the gecko, on the other hand, represents immobile concentration and the hidden side, the obverse of what is displayed to the eye.

The most extraordinary thing are the claws, actual hands with soft fingers, all pad, which, pressed against the glass, adhere to it with their minuscule suckers: the five fingers stretch out like the petals of little flowers in a childish drawing, and when one claw moves, the fingers close like a flower, only to spread out again and flatten against the glass, making tiny streaks, like fingerprints. At once delicate and strong, these hands seem to contain a potential intelligence, so that if they could only be freed from their task of remaining stuck there to the vertical surface they could acquire the talents of human hands, which are said to have become skilled after they no longer had to cling to boughs or press on the ground.

Bent, the legs seem not so much all knee as all elbow, elastic in order to raise the body. The tail adheres to the glass only along a central strip, from which the rings begin that circle it from one side to the other and make of it a sturdy and well-protected implement; most of the time it is listless, idle, and seems to have no talent or ambition beyond subsidiary support (nothing like the calligraphic agility of lizards' tails); but when called upon, it proves well-articulated, ready to react, even expressive.

Of the head, the vibrant, capacious gullet is visible, and the protruding, lidless eyes at either side. The throat is a limp sack's surface extending from the tip of the chin, hard and all scales like that of an alligator, to the white belly that, where it presses against the glass, also reveals a grainy, perhaps adhesive, speckling.

When a gnat passes close to the gecko's throat, the tongue flicks and engulfs, rapid and supple and prehensile, without shape, capable of assuming whatever shape. In any case, Mr Palomar is never sure if he has seen it or not seen it: what he surely does see, now, is the gnat inside the reptile's gullet: the belly pressed against the illuminated glass is transparent as if under X-rays; you can follow the shadow of the prey in its course through the viscera that absorb it.

If all material were transparent – the ground that supports us, the envelope that sheathes our body – everything would be seen not as a fluttering of impalpable wings but as an inferno of grinding and ingesting. Perhaps at this moment a god of the nether world situated in the center of the earth with his eye that can pierce granite is watching us from below, following the cycle of living and dying, the lacerated victims dissolving in the bellies of their devourers until they, in their turn, are swallowed by another belly.

The gecko remains motionless for hours; with a snap of his tongue he gulps down a mosquito or a gnat every now and then; other insects, on the contrary, identical to the first, light unawares a few millimeters from his mouth and he seems not to perceive them. Is it the vertical pupil of his eyes, separated at the sides of his head, that does not notice? Or does he have criteria of choice and rejection that we do not know? Or are his actions prompted by chance or by whim?

The segmentation of legs and tail into rings, the speckling of tiny granulous plates on his head and belly give the gecko the appearance of a mechanical device; a highly elaborate machine, its every microscopic detail carefully studied, so that you begin to wonder if all that perfection is not squandered, in view of the limited operations it performs. Or is this perhaps the secret: content to be, does he reduce his doing to the minimum? Can this be his lesson, the opposite of the morality that, in his youth, Mr Palomar wanted to make his: to strive always to do something a bit beyond one's means?

Now a bewildered nocturnal butterfly comes within range. Will he overlook it? No, he catches this, too. His tongue is transformed into a butterfly net and he pulls it into his mouth. Will it all fit? Will he spit it out? Will he explode? No, the butterfly is there in his throat: it flutters, in a sorry state, but still itself, not touched by the insult of chewing teeth, now it passes the narrow limits of the neck, it is a shadow that begins its slow and troubled journey down along a swollen esophagus.

The gecko, emerging from its impassiveness, gasps, shakes its convulsed throat, staggers on legs and tail, twists its belly, subjected to a severe test. Will this be enough for him, for tonight? Will he go away? Was this the peak of every desire he yearned to satisfy? Was this the nearly impossible test in which he wanted to prove himself? No, he stays. Perhaps he has fallen asleep. What is sleep like for someone who has eyes without eyelids?

Mr Palomar is unable to move from there either. He sits and stares at the gecko. There is no truce on which he can count. Even if he turned the television back on, he would only be extending the contemplation of massacres. The butterfly, fragile Eurydice, sinks slowly into her Hades. A gnat flies, is about to light on the glass. And the gecko's tongue whips out.

The invasion of the starlings

There is something extraordinary to be seen in Rome in this late autumn and it is the sky crammed with birds. Mr Palomar's terrace is a good observation post; from it his gaze roves over roofs along a broad circle of horizon. Of these birds he knows only what he has heard people saying: they are starlings, which gather by the hundreds of thousands, coming from the north, waiting until it is time for them to leave all together for the coasts of Africa. At night they sleep on the city's trees, and anyone who parks his car on the street along the Tiber is obliged to wash it the next morning from stem to stern.

Where do they go during the day? What function does this prolonged stop-over in one city have in the strategy of their migration? What meaning do these immense evening assemblies have for them, this aerial pageant like a parade or the great annual maneuvers? Mr Palomar still has not managed to understand. The explanations offered are all a bit dubious, conditioned by hypotheses, wavering among various alternatives; and this is only natural, since these are rumors that pass from mouth to mouth, but even science, which should confirm or deny them, is apparently uncertain, approximate. Things being as they are then, Mr Palomar has decided to confine himself to watching, to establishing down to the slightest detail what little he manages to see, sticking to the immediate ideas that what he sees suggests.

In the violet sunset air he watches a very minute dust surface from one part of the sky, a cloud of flying wings. He realizes that they are thousands and thousands: the dome of the sky is invaded. What had seemed so far a serene and empty immensity proves to be all traversed by very rapid and light presences.

A reassuring sight, the passage of migratory birds is associated in our ancestral memory with the harmonious succession of the seasons; instead, Mr Palomar feels something akin to apprehension. Can it be because this crowding of the sky reminds us that the balance of nature has been lost? Or is it because our sense of insecurity finds threats of catastrophe everywhere?

When you think of migratory birds you usually imagine a very orderly and compact flight formation, which furrows the sky in a long host or a right-angled phalanx, like a bird-shape made up of countless birds. This image does not apply to the starlings, or at least not to these autumnal starlings in the Roman sky: this is an airy crowd that seems always about to scatter and disperse, like grains of a powder suspended in a liquid; instead, it thickens constantly as if from an invisible conduit the jet of whirling particles continues, never managing, however, to saturate the solution.

The cloud spreads, blackening with wings outlined more sharply in the sky, a sign that they are approaching. Inside the flock Mr Palomar can already discern a perspective, for he sees some of the birds already very near, over his head, others far off, others farther still, and he continues discovering more, tinier and punctiform, for kilometers and kilometers, you would say, attributing to the distances between one and another an almost equal length. But this illusion of regularity is treacherous, because nothing is more difficult to evaluate than the density of distribution of birds in flight, where the compactness of the flock seems about to darken the sky. There, between one winged animal and the next, chasms of emptiness yawn.

If he lingers for a few moments to observe the arrangement of the birds, one in relation to the other, Mr Palomar feels caught in a weft whose continuity extends, uniform and without rents, as if he also were part of this moving body composed of hundreds and hundreds of bodies, detached, but forming together a single object, like a cloud or a column of smoke or a jet of water, something, in other words, which even in the fluidity of its substance achieves a formal solidity of its own. But he has only to start following a single bird with his gaze and the disassociation of the elements regains the upper hand and the current which he felt transporting him, the network which he felt sustaining him, dissolve, and the effect is that of a vertigo that grips him at the pit of the stomach.

This happens, for example, when Mr Palomar, after having convinced himself that the flock as a whole is flying towards him, directs his gaze to a bird that is, on the contrary, moving away, and from this one to another, also moving away but in a different direction; and he soon notices that all the birds that seemed to him to be approaching are in reality flying off in all directions, as if he were in the center of an explosion. But he has only to turn his eyes towards another zone of the sky and there they are, concentrated over there, in an increasingly thick and crammed vortex, as when a magnet hidden under a sheet of paper attracts iron filings, making patterns that become darker one moment, lighter the next, and in the end dissolve and leave on the white page a speckling of scattered fragments.

Finally a form emerges from the confused flutter of wings, it advances, condenses: it is a circular shape, like a sphere, a bubble, the balloon-speech of someone who is thinking of a sky full of birds, an avalanche of wings that rolls in the air and involves all the birds flying in the vicinity. This sphere, in the uniform space, represents a special territory, a moving volume within whose confines – which still dilate and contract like an elastic surface – the flocks can go on flying, each in its own direction provided they do not alter the circular shape of the whole.

At a certain point Mr Palomar realizes that the number of whirling creatures inside the globe is rapidly increasing as if a very swift current were decanting there a new population with the speed of sand in an hourglass. It is another gust of starlings that also assumes a spherical form, spreading out within the preceding form. But the cohesion of the flock does not seem to resist beyond certain dimensions: in fact, Mr Palomar is already observing a dispersion of birds at the edges, or rather, real gaps open and begin to deflate the sphere. He barely has time to notice it before the pattern has dissolved.

Mr Palomar's observations on birds succeed one another and multiply at such a pace that Mr Palomar feels the need to communicate them to his friends. His friends also have something to say on the subject, because each of them has happened to take some interest in the phenomenon already or else because some interest has been awakened in them after Mr Palomar has talked to them. It is a subject that can never be considered exhausted and when one of the friends believes he has seen something new or feels called upon to rectify a previous impression, he seems obliged to telephone the others at once. And so there is a to and fro of messages along the telephone network as the sky is criss-crossed by hosts of birds.

"Have you noticed how they manage to avoid one another even when they are flying closest together, even when their paths intersect? You'd think they have radar."

"That's not so. I've found lots of birds on the pavement, battered or dying or dead. They're the victims of collisions in flight, inevitable when the density is too great."

"I've figured out why they keep flying all together in the evening over this area of the city. They're like planes stacked up over the airport, circling until they get a permission-to-land signal. That's why we see them flying around for such a long time; they're waiting their turn to perch on the trees where they will spend the night."

"I've seen how they act when they light on the trees. They fly around and around in the sky, in a spiral, then one by one they dive very fast towards their chosen tree, then they brake sharply and light on the branch."

"No, aerial traffic jams can't be a problem. Each bird has a tree that is his, he has his branch and his place on the branch. He can pick it out from above and he dives."

"Is their eyesight so sharp?"

"Hmph."

The phone-calls are never long, because Mr Palomar is also impatient to get back to the terrace, as if he were afraid of missing some decisive turn of events.

Now you would say that the birds occupy only that portion of the sky that is still struck by the rays of the setting sun. But taking a better look, you realize that the condensing and thinning out of the birds unwinds like a long ribbon, flapping in a zigzag. Where this ribbon curves the flock seems thicker, like a swarm of bees; where it stretches out, not twisting, there is only a dotting of scattered flights.

Until the last glow vanishes in the sky, and a tide of darkness rises from the depths of the streets to submerge the archipelago of tiles and domes and terraces and garrets and loggias and spires; and the suspension of the black wings of the celestial invaders precipitates until it is confused with the grievous flight of the stupid, spattering urban pigeons.

PALOMAR DOES THE SHOPPING

Two pounds of goose-fat

The goose-fat is shown in glass jars, each containing, as the handwritten label says, "two limbs of plump goose (a leg and a wing), goose-fat, salt and pepper. Net weight: two pounds." In the thick, soft whiteness that fills the jars the clangor of the world is muffled: a dark shadow rises from the bottom and, as in the fog of memories, allows a glimpse of the goose's severed limbs, lost in its fat.

Mr Palomar is standing in line in a Paris charcuterie. It is the holiday season, but here the throng of customers is usual even at less ceremonial times, because this is one of the good gastronomical shops of the city, miraculously surviving in a neighborhood where the leveling of mass trade, taxes, the low income of the consumers, and now the depression have dismantled the old shops, one by one, replacing them with anonymous supermarkets.

Waiting in line, Mr Palomar contemplates the jars. He tries to find a place in his memories for *cassoulet*, a rich stew of meats and beans, in which goose-fat is an essential ingredient; but neither his palate's memory nor his cultural memory is of any help to him. And yet the name, the sight, the idea attract him, awaken an immediate fantasy not so much of appetite as of eros: from a mountain of goose-fat a female figure surfaces, smears white over her rosy skin, and he already imagines himself making his way towards her through those thick avalanches, embracing her, sinking with her.

He dispels this incongruous thought from his mind, raises his eyes to the ceiling bedecked with salamis, hanging from the Christmas wreaths like fruit from boughs in the land of Cockaigne. All around, on the marble counters, abundance triumphs in the forms developed by civilization and art. In the slices of game pâté, the pursuits and flights of the moor are fixed forever, sublimated in a tapestry of flavors. The galantines of pheasant are arrayed in gray-pink cylinders surmounted, to certify their origin, by two birdly feet like talons that jut from a coat-of-arms or from a Renaissance chest.

Through the gelatine sheaths the thick beauty-spots of black truffle stand out, aligned like buttons on a Pierrot's tunic, like the notes of a score, dotting the roseate, variegated beds of pâtés de foie gras, of head-cheese, terrines, galantines, fans of salmon, artichoke hearts garnished like trophies. The leading motive of the little truffle discs unifies the variety of substances like the black of dinner-jackets at a masked ball, distinguishing the festive dress of the foods.

Gray and opaque and sullen, on the contrary, are the people who make their way among the counters, shunted by salesladies in white, more or less elderly, brusquely efficient. The splendor of the salmon canapés radiant with mayonnaise disappears, swallowed by the dark shopping-bags of the customers. Certainly every one of these men and women knows exactly what he wants, heads straight for his objective with a decisiveness admitting no hesitancy; and rapidly he dismantles mountains of vol-au-vents, white puddings, cervelats.

Mr Palomar would like to catch in their eyes some reflection of those treasures' spell, but the faces and actions are only impatient and hasty, of people concentrated on themselves, nerves taut, each concerned with what he has and what he does not have. Nobody seems to him worthy of the pantagruelian glory that unfolds in those cases, on the counters. A greed without joy or youth drives them; and yet a deep, atavistic bond exists between them and those foods, their consubstance, flesh of their flesh.

He realizes he is feeling something closely akin to jealousy: he would like the duck and hare pâtés, from their platters, to show they prefer him to the others, recognizing him as the only one deserving of their gifts, those gifts that nature and culture have handed down for millennia and that must not now fall into profane hands! Is not the sacred enthusiasm that he feels pervading him perhaps a sign that he alone is the elect, the one touched by grace, the only one worthy of the deluge of good things brimming from the cornucopia of the world?

He looks around, waiting to hear the vibration of an orchestra of flavors. No, nothing vibrates. All those delicacies stir in him imprecise, blurred memories; his imagination does not instinctively associate flavors with images and names. He asks himself if his gluttony is not chiefly mental, aesthetic, symbolic. Perhaps, for all the sincerity of his love of galantines, galantines do not love him. They sense that his gaze transforms every food into a document of the history of civilization, a museum exhibit.

Mr Palomar wishes the line would advance more rapidly. He knows that if he spends a few more hours in this shop, he will end up convincing himself that he is the profane one, the alien, the outsider.

The cheese museum

Mr Palomar is standing in line in a cheese shop, in Paris. He wants to buy certain goat cheeses that are preserved in oil in little transparent containers and spiced with various herbs and condiments. The line of customers moves along a counter where samples of the most unusual and disparate specialties are displayed. This is a shop whose range seems meant to document every conceivable form of dairy product; the very sign, "*Spécialités froumagères,*" with that rare archaic or vernacular adjective, advises that here is guarded the legacy of a knowledge accumulated by a civilization through all its history and geography.

Three or four girls in pink smocks wait on the customers. The moment one of the girls is free she deals with the first in line and asks him to express his wishes; the customer names or, more often, points, moving about the shop towards the object of his specific and expert appetites.

At that moment the whole line moves forward one place; and the person who till then had been standing beside the "Bleu d'Auvergne" veined with green now finds himself at the level of the "Brin d'amour", whose whiteness holds strands of dried straw stuck to it; the customer contemplating a ball wrapped in leaves can now concentrate on a cube dusted with ash. At each move forward, some customers are inspired by new stimuli and new desires: they may change their minds about what they were about to ask for or may add a new item to the list; and there are also those who never allow themselves to be distracted even for a moment from the objective they are pursuing – every different, fortuitous suggestion serves only to limit, through exclusion, the field of what they stubbornly want.

Palomar's spirit vacillates between contrasting urges: the one that aims at complete, exhaustive knowledge and could be satisfied only by tasting all the varieties; and the one that tends towards an absolute choice, the identification of the cheese that is his alone, a cheese that certainly exists even if he cannot recognize it (cannot recognize himself in it).

Or else, or else: it is not a matter of choosing the right cheese, but of being chosen. There is a reciprocal relationship between cheese and customer: each cheese awaits its customer, poses so as to attract him, with a firmness or a somewhat haughty graininess, or on the contrary, by melting in submissive abandon.

There is a hint of complicity hovering in the air: the refinement of the taste buds, and especially of the olfactory organs, has its moments of weakness, of loss of class, when the cheeses on their platters seem to proffer themselves as if on the divans of a brothel. A perverse grin flickers in the satisfaction of debasing the object of one's own gluttony with lowering nicknames: *crottin, boule de moine, bouton de culotte.*

This is not the kind of acquaintance that Mr Palomar is most inclined to pursue: he would be content to establish the simplicity of a direct physical relationship between man and cheese. But as in place of the cheeses he sees names of cheeses, concepts of cheeses, meanings of cheeses, histories of cheeses, contexts of cheeses, psychologies of cheeses, when he does not so much know as sense that behind each of these cheeses there is all that, then his relationship becomes very complicated.

The cheese shop appears to Palomar the way an encyclopedia looks to an autodidact; he could memorize all the names, venture a classification according to the forms – cake of soap, cylinder, dome, ball – according to the consistency – dry, buttery, creamy, veined, firm – according to the alien materials involved in the crust or in the heart – raisins, pepper, walnuts, sesame seeds, herbs, molds – but this would not bring him a step closer to true knowledge, which lies in the experience of the flavors, composed of memory and imagination at once. Only on the basis of that could he establish a scale of preferences and tastes and curiosities and exclusions.

Behind every cheese there is a pasture of a different green under a different sky: meadows caked with salt that the tides of Normandy deposit every evening; meadows scented with aromas in the windy sunlight of Provence; there are different flocks with their stablings and their transhumances; there are secret processes handed down over the centuries. This shop is a museum: Mr Palomar, visiting it, feels, as he does in the Louvre, behind every displayed object the presence of the civilization that has given it form and takes form from it.

This shop is a dictionary; the language is the system of cheeses as a whole: a language whose morphology records declensions and conjugations in countless variants, and whose lexicon presents an inexhaustible richness of synonyms, idiomatic usages, connotations and nuances of meaning, as in all languages nourished by the contribution of a hundred dialects. It is a language made up of things; its nomenclature is only an external aspect, instrumental; but, for Mr Palomar, learning a bit of nomenclature remains still the first measure to be taken if he wants to stop for a moment the things that are flowing before his eyes.

From his pocket he takes a notebook, a pen, begins to write down some names, marking beside each name some feature that will enable him to recall the image to his memory; he tries also to make a synthetic sketch of the shape. He writes "Pavé d'Airvault" and notes "green mold", draws a flat parallelopiped and to one side notes "4cm. circa"; he writes "St-Maure", notes "gray granular cylinder with a little shaft inside" and draws it, measuring it at a glance as about "20 cm."; then he writes "Chabicholi" and draws another little cylinder.

"*Monsieur! Hoo there! Monsieur!*" A young cheese-girl, dressed in pink, is standing in front of him, as he is occupied with his notebook. It is his turn, he is next; in the line behind him everyone is observing his incongruous behavior, heads are being shaken with those half-ironic, half-exasperated looks with which the inhabitants of the big cities consider the ever-increasing number of the mentally retarded wandering about the streets.

The elaborate and greedy order that he intended to make momentarily slips his mind; he stammers; he falls back on the most obvious, the most banal, the most advertised, as if the automatons of mass civilization were waiting only for this moment of uncertainty on his part in order to seize him again and have him at their mercy.

Marble and blood

The reflections the butcher's shop inspires in someone entering with a shopping-bag involve information handed down for centuries in various branches of learning: expertise in meats and cuts, the best way of cooking each piece, the rites that allay remorse at the ending of other lives in order to sustain one's own. Butchering wisdom and culinary learning belong to the exact sciences, which can be checked through experimentation, bearing in mind the habits and techniques that vary from one country to another; sacrificial learning, on the other hand, is dominated by uncertainty, and moreover, it fell into oblivion centuries ago, but still it weighs obscurely on the conscience, an unexpressed demand. A reverent devotion for everything that concerns meat guides Mr Palomar, who is preparing to buy three steaks. Amid the marble slabs of the butcher's shop he stands as if in a temple, aware that his individual existence and the culture to which he belongs are conditioned by this place.

The line of customers moves slowly along the high marble counter, past the shelves and the trays where the cuts of meat are aligned, each with its name and price on a tag stuck into it. The vivid red of the beef precedes the light pink of the veal, the dull red of the lamb, the dark red of the pork. Vast ribs blaze up, round tournedos whose thickness is lined by a ribbon of lard, slender and agile counter-filets, steaks armed with their invincible bone, massive rolled-roasts all lean, chunks for boiling with layers of fat and of red meat, roasts waiting for the string that will force them to enfold themselves; then the colors fade: veal escalopes, loin chops, pieces of shoulder and breast, cartilage; and then we enter the realm of legs and shoulders of lamb; farther on some white tripe glows, a liver glistens blackly . . .

Behind the counter, the white-smocked butchers brandish their cleavers with the trapezoidal blade, their great knives for slicing and those for flaying, saws for severing bones, pounders with which they press the snaky pink curls into the funnel of the grinding machine. From hooks hang quartered carcases to remind you that your every morsel is part of a being whose living completeness has been arbitrarily torn asunder.

On the wall a chart shows an outline of a bull, like a map covered with frontier lines that mark off the areas of consuming interest, involving the entire anatomy of the animal excepting only horns and hooves. The map of the human habitat is this, no less than the planisphere of the planet; both are protocols that should sanction the rights man has attributed to himself, of possession, division, and consumption without residue of the terrestrial continents and of the loins of the animal body.

It must be said that the man–beef symbiosis has, over the centuries, achieved an equilibrium (allowing the two species to continue multiplying) though it is asymmetric (it is true that man takes care of feeding cattle, but he is not required to give them himself to feed on), and has guaranteed the flourishing of what is called human civilization, which at least in part should be called human–bovine (coinciding in part with the human–ovine and in smaller part with the human–porcine, depending on the alternatives of a complicated geography of religious prohibitions). Mr Palomar shares in this symbiosis with a clear conscience and full agreement: though he recognizes in the strung-up carcase of the beef the person of a disemboweled brother, and in the slash of the loin chop the wound that mutilates his own flesh, he knows that he is a carnivore, conditioned by his alimentary background to perceive in a butcher's shop the premiss of gustatory happiness, to imagine, observing these reddish slices, the stripes that the flame will leave on the grilled steaks and the pleasure of the tooth in severing the browned fiber.

One sentiment does not exclude another: Mr Palomar's mood as he stands in line in the butcher's shop is at once of restrained joy and of fear, desire and respect, egotistic concern and universal compassion, the mood that perhaps others express in prayer.

PALOMAR AT THE ZOO

The giraffe race

Visiting the Vincennes zoo, Mr Palomar stops at the giraffes' yard. Every now and then the adult giraffes start running, followed by the baby giraffes; they charge almost to the fence, wheel around, repeat the dash two or three times, then stop. Mr Palomar never tires of watching the giraffes' race, fascinated by their unharmonious movements. He cannot decide whether they are galloping or trotting, because the stride of their hind legs has nothing in common with that of their forelegs. The forelegs arch loosely to the breast, then unfold to the ground, as if unsure which of numerous articulations they should employ at that given moment. The hind legs, much shorter and stiff, follow in leaps and bounds, somewhat obliquely, as if they were of wood, or crutches stumbling along, but also as if playing, aware of being comical. Meanwhile the outstretched neck sways up and down, like the arm of a crane, with no possible relationship between the movement of the legs and the movement of the neck. The withers also give a jolt, but this is simply the movement of the neck that jerks the rest of the spinal column.

The giraffe seems a mechanism constructed by putting together pieces from heterogeneous machines, though it functions perfectly all the same. Mr Palomar, as he continues observing the racing giraffes, becomes aware of a complicated harmony that commands that unharmonious trampling, an

inner proportion that links the most glaring anatomical
disproportions, a natural grace that emerges from those
ungraceful movements. The unifying element comes from
the spots on the hide, arranged in irregular but homogeneous
patterns: they agree, like a precise graphic equivalent, with
the animal's segmented movements. The hide should not be
considered spotted, but rather a black coat whose uniformity
is broken by pale veins that open in a lozenge design: an
unevenness of pigmentation that preannounces the unevenness of the movements.

At this point Mr Palomar's little girl, who has long since
tired of watching the giraffes, pulls him towards the penguins'
cave. Mr Palomar, in whom penguins inspire anguish, follows
her reluctantly and asks himself why he is so interested in
giraffes. Perhaps because the world around him moves in an
unharmonious way, and he hopes always to find some pattern
in it, a constant. Perhaps because he himself feels that his own
advance is impelled by uncoordinated movements of the
mind, which seem to have nothing to do with one another
and are increasingly difficult to fit into any pattern of inner
harmony.

The albino gorilla

In the Barcelona zoo there exists the only example known in the world of the great albino ape, a gorilla from equatorial Africa. Mr Palomar picks his way through the crowd that presses into the animal's building. Beyond a sheet of plate glass, "Copito de Nieve" ("Snowflake", as they call him), is a mountain of flesh and white hide. Seated against a wall, he is taking the sun. The facial mask is a human pink, carved by wrinkles; the chest also reveals a pink and glabrous skin, like that of a human of the white race. With its enormous features, a sad giant's, that face turns every now and then towards the crowd of visitors beyond the glass, less than a meter from him, a slow gaze charged with desolation and patience and boredom, a gaze that expresses all the resignation at being the way he is, sole exemplar in the world of a form not chosen, not loved, all the effort of bearing his own singlarity, and the suffering at occupying space and time with his presence so cumbersome and evident.

The glass looks on to an enclosure surrounded by high masonry walls, which give it the appearance of a prison yard but actually it is the "garden" of the gorilla's house-cage; from its soil rises a short, leafless tree and an iron ladder like those in a gymnasium. Farther back in the yard there is the female, a great black gorilla carrying a baby in her arms: the whiteness of the coat cannot be inherited, "Copito de Nieve" remains the only albino of all gorillas.

White and motionless, the great ape suggests to Mr Palomar's mind an immemorial antiquity, like mountains or like the pyramids. In reality the animal is still young and only the contrast between the pink face and the short snow coat that frames it and, especially, the wrinkles all around the eyes give him the look of an old man. For the rest, the appearance of "Copito de Nieve" shows fewer resemblances to humans than that of other primates: in place of a nose, the nostrils dig a double chasm; the hands, hairy and – it would seem – not very highly articulated, at the end of the very long and stiff arms, are actually still paws, and the gorilla uses them as such when he walks, pressing them to the ground like a quadruped.

Now these arm-paws are pressing a rubber tire against his chest. In the enormous void of his hours, "Copito de Nieve" never abandons the tire. What can this object be for him? A toy? A fetish? A talisman? Palomar feels he understands the gorilla perfectly, his need for something to hold tight while everything eludes him, a thing with which to allay the anguish of isolation, of difference, of the sentence to being always considered a living phenomenon, not only by the visitors to the zoo but also by his own females and his children.

The female also has an old tire, but for her it is an object of normal use, with which she has a practical relationship, without problems: she sits in it as if it were an easychair, sun-bathing and de-lousing her infant. For "Copito de Nieve", on the contrary, the contact with the tire seems to be something affective, possessive, and somehow symbolic. From it he can have a glimpse of what for man is the search for an escape from the dismay of living: investing oneself in things, recognizing oneself in signs, transforming the world into a collection of symbols; a first daybreak of culture in the long biological night. To do this the gorilla possesses only an old tire, an artefact of human production, alien to him, lacking any symbolic potentiality, naked of meanings, abstract. Looking at it, you would not say that much could be derived from it. And yet what, more than an empty circle, can contain all the symbols you might want to attribute to it? Perhaps identifying himself with it, the gorilla is about to reach, in the depths of silence, the springs from which language burst forth, to establish a flow of relationships between his thoughts and the unyielding, deaf evidence of the facts that determine his life . . .

Leaving the zoo, Mr Palomar cannot dispel the image of the albino gorilla from his mind. He tries to talk about him with people he meets, but he cannot make anyone listen to him. At night, both during the hours of insomnia and during his brief dreams, the great ape continues to appear to him. "Just as the gorilla has his tire, which serves as tangible support for a raving, wordless speech," he thinks, "so I have this image of a great white ape. We all turn in our hands an old, empty tire through which we would like to reach the final meaning, at which words do not arrive."

The order of scaly creatures

Mr Palomar would like to know why iguanas attract him. In Paris he goes now and then to visit the reptile house of the Jardin des Plantes; he is never disappointed. What is extraordinary, indeed unique, about the appearance of the iguana in itself is quite clear to him; but he feels there is something more and he cannot say what it is.

The *Iguana iguana* is covered with a green skin that seems woven from very tiny speckled scales. There is too much of this skin: on the neck, on the legs, it forms folds, bags, flounces, like a dress that should adhere to the body and instead sags on all sides. Along the spinal column there is a jagged crest that extends to the tail; the tail is also green up to a point, after which the farther it stretches the paler it becomes, and it is divided into rings of alternating colors: light brown and dark brown. On the scaly green snout, the eye opens and closes, and this is an "evolved" eye, endowed with gaze, attention, sadness, suggesting that another being is concealed inside that dragon semblance: an animal more similar to those we are at home with, a living presence less distant from us than it seems . . .

Then there are other spiky crests under the chin; on the neck there are two round white plates like a hearing-aid; a number of accessories and sundries, trimmings and defensive garnishings, a sample-case of forms available in the animal kingdom and perhaps also in other kingdoms: too much stuff for one animal to bear. What's the use of it? Does it serve to disguise someone watching us from in there?

The forelegs, with five fingers, would suggest talons rather than hands if they were not attached to actual arms, muscular and well-shaped; but the rear legs are different, long and flabby, with fingers like vegetable propagations. The animal as a whole, however, even from the depths of his resigned, motionless torpor, conveys an image of strength.

At the glass case of the *Iguana iguana* Mr Palomar has stopped, after having contemplated the case with ten little iguanas clinging one to the other, constantly shifting position with agile movements of elbows and knees, all stretching in a lengthwise direction: the skin a brilliant green, with a copper-colored dot in the place of gills, a crested white beard, pale eyes wide around the black pupil. Then the Squirrel of the Savannah, which hides in sand its identical color; the Tegu or Tupinambis, yellowish-black, almost an alligator; the giant African Cordilo, with thick, pointed scales like fur or leaves, the color of the desert, so concentrated in its determination to exclude itself from the world that it coils in a circle, curling its tail against its head. The gray-green upper shell and the white underneath of a turtle immersed in the water of a transparent tank seem soft, fleshy; the pointed head emerges as if from a high collar.

Life in the snake house appears a squandering of forms without style and without plan, where all is possible, and animals and plants and rocks exchange scales, quills, concretions. But among the infinite possible combinations only some – perhaps actually the most incredible – become fixed, resist the flux that undoes them and mixes and reshapes; and immediately each of these forms becomes the center of a world, separated forever from the others, as here in the row of glass case-cages of the zoo; and in this finite number of ways of being, each identified in a monstrosity of its own, and necessity, and beauty of its own, lies order, the sole order recognizable in the world. The iguana room of the Jardin des Plantes, with its illuminated cases, where dozing reptiles are hidden among branches and rocks and sand of the forest or the desert of their origin, reflects the order of the world, whether it be the reflection on earth of the sky of ideas or the external manifestation of the secret of the nature of creation, of the norm concealed in the depths of that which exists.

Is it this atmosphere, more than the reptiles in themselves, that obscurely attracts Mr Palomar? A damp, soft warmth soaks the air like a sponge; a sharp stink, heavy, rotten, forces him to hold his breath; shadow and light lie stagnant in a motionless mixture of days and nights: are these the sensations of a man who peers out beyond the human? Beyond the glass of every cage there is the world as it was before man, or after, to show that the world of man is not eternal and is not unique. Is it to realize this with his own eyes that Mr Palomar reviews these stalls where pythons sleep, boas, bamboo rattlesnakes, the tree-adder of the Bermudas?

But of the worlds from which man is excluded each case is only a tiny sample, torn from a natural continuum that might also never have existed, a few cubic meters of atmosphere that elaborate devices maintain at a certain degree of temperature and humidity. Thus every sample of this antediluvian bestiary is kept alive artificially, as if it were a hypothesis of the mind, a product of the imagination, a construction of language, a paradoxical line of reasoning meant to demonstrate that the only true world is our own . . .

As if the smell of the reptiles were only now becoming unbearable, Mr Palomar suddenly feels a desire to go out into the open air. He has to cross the great hall of the crocodiles, where there is a line of tanks separated by barriers. In the dry part beside each tank lie the crocodiles, alone or in couples, a spent color, squat, rough, horrible, heavily stretched out, flattened against the ground the full length of their long, cruel snouts, their cold bellies, their broad tails. They all seem asleep, even those whose eyes are open, or perhaps all are sleepless in a dazed desolation, even with their eyes closed. From time to time one of them stirs slowly, barely raises himself on his short legs, crawls to the edge of the tank, lets himself drop with a flat thud, raising a wave. He floats, immersed in the water, as motionless as before. Is theirs a boundless patience, or a desperation without end? What are they waiting for, or what have they given up waiting for? In what time are they immersed? In that of the species, removed from the course of the hours that race from the birth to the death of the individual? Or in the time of geological eras that shifts continents and solidifies the crust of emerged lands? Or in the slow cooling of the rays of the sun? The thought of a time outside our experience is intolerable. Palomar hurries to leave the snake house, which can be visited only now and then and in haste.

THE SILENCES OF
PALOMAR

The sand garden

A little courtyard covered with a white sand, thick-grained, almost gravel, raked in straight, parallel furrows or in concentric circles, around five irregular groups of stones or low boulders. This is one of the most famous monuments of Japanese civilization, the garden of rocks and sand of the Ryoanji of Kyoto, the image typical of that contemplation of the absolute to be achieved with the simplest means and without recourse to concepts capable of verbal expression, according to the teaching of the Zen monks, the most spiritual of Buddhist sects.

The rectangular enclosure of colorless sand is flanked on three sides by walls surmounted by tiles, beyond which is the green of trees. On the fourth side there is a wooden platform, of steps, where the public can file by or linger and sit down. "If our inner gaze remains absorbed in the viewing of this garden," explains the pamphlet offered visitors, in Japanese and in English, signed by the abbot of the temple, "we will feel divested of the relativity of our individual ego, whereas the sense of the absolute *I* will fill us with serene wonder purifying our clouded minds."

Mr Palomar is prepared to accept this advice on faith, and he sits on the steps, observes the rocks one by one, follows the undulations of the white sand, allows the indefinable harmony that links the elements of the picture gradually to pervade him.

Or rather, he tries to imagine all these things as they would be felt by someone who could concentrate on looking at the Zen garden in solitude and silence. Because – we had forgotten to say – Mr Palomar is crammed on the platform in the midst of hundreds of visitors, who jostle him on every side; camera-lenses and movie-cameras force their way past the elbows, knees, ears of the crowd, to frame the rocks and the sand from every angle, illuminated by natural light or by flashbulbs. Swarms of feet in wool socks step over him (shoes, as always in Japan, are left at the entrance); numerous offspring are thrust to the front row by pedagogical parents; clumps of uniformed students shove one another, eager only to conclude as quickly as possible this school outing to the famous monument; earnest visitors nodding their heads rhythmically check and make sure that everything written in the guidebook corresponds to reality and that everything seen in reality is also mentioned in the guide.

"We can view the garden as a group of mountainous islands in a great ocean, or as mountain tops rising above a sea of clouds. We can see it as a picture framed by the ancient mud walls, or we can forget the frame as we sense the truth of this sea stretching out boundlessly."

These "instructions for use" are contained in the leaflet, and to Mr Palomar they seem perfectly plausible and immediately applicable, without effort, provided one is really sure of having a personality to shed, of looking at the world from inside an ego that can be dissolved, to become only a gaze. But it is precisely this outset that demands an effort of supplementary imagination, very difficult to muster when one's ego is glued into a solid crowd looking through its thousand eyes and walking on its thousand feet along the established itinerary of the tourist visit.

Must the conclusion be that the Zen mental techniques for achieving extreme humility, detachment from all possessiveness and pride require as their necessary background aristocratic privilege, and assume an individualism with so much space and so much time around it, the horizons of a solitude free of anguish?

But this conclusion, which leads to the familiar lament over a paradise lost in the spread of mass civilization, sounds too facile for Mr Palomar. He prefers to take a more difficult path, to try to grasp what the Zen garden can give him, looking at it in the only situation in which it can be looked at today, craning his neck among other necks.

What does he see? He sees the human race in the era of great numbers, which extends in a crowd, leveled but still made up of distinct individualities like the sea of grains of sand that submerges the surface of the world . . . He sees that the world, nevertheless, continues to turn the boulder-back of its nature indifferent to the fate of mankind, its hard substance that cannot be reduced to human assimilation . . . He sees the forms in which the assembled human sand tends to arrange itself along lines of movement, patterns that combine regularity and fluidity like the rectilinear or circular tracks of a rake . . . And between mankind—sand and world—boulder there is a sense of possible harmony, as if between two non-homogeneous harmonies: that of the non-human in a balance of forces that seems not to correspond to any pattern, and that of human structures, which aspires to the rationality of a geometrical or musical composition, never definitive . . .

Serpents and skulls

In Mexico, Mr Palomar is visiting the ruins of Tula, ancient capital of the Toltecs. A Mexican friend accompanies him, an impassioned and eloquent expert on pre-Columbian civilizations, who tells him beautiful legends about Quetzalcoatl. Before becoming a god, Quetzalcoatl was a king, with his palace here in Tula; a line of lopped-off columns remains, around an impluvium, a bit like a palace of ancient Rome.

The temple of the Morning Star is a step-pyramid. At the top stand four cylindrical caryatids, known as "Atlases", who represent the god Quetzalcoatl as the Morning Star (through a butterfly they bear on their back, symbol of the star), and four carved columns, which represent the Plumed Serpent, the same god in animal form.

All this has to be taken on faith; for that matter, it would be hard to demonstrate the opposite. In Mexican archeology every statue, every object, every detail of a bas-relief stands for something that stands for something else that stands, in turn, for yet another something. An animal stands for a god who stands for a star that stands for an element or a human quality and so on. We are in the world of pictographic writing; the ancient Mexicans, to write, drew pictures, and even when they were drawing it was as if they were writing: every picture seems a rebus to be deciphered. Even the most abstract, geometric friezes on the wall of a temple can be interpreted as arrows if you see a motive of broken lines, or you can read a numerical sequence, depending on the way the key-pattern is repeated. Here in Tula the reliefs depict stylized animal forms: jaguars, coyotes. Mr Palomar's Mexican friend pauses at each stone, transforms it into a cosmic tale, an allegory, a moral reflection.

A group of schoolchildren moves among the ruins: stocky boys with the features of the Indios, descendants perhaps of the builders of these temples, wearing a plain white uniform, like Boy Scouts, with blue neckerchiefs. The boys are led by a teacher not much taller than they are and only a little more adult, with the same round, dark, impassive face. They climb the top steps of the pyramid, stop beneath the columns, the teacher tells what civilization they belong to, what century, what stone they are carved from, then concludes, "We don't know what they mean," and the group follows him down the steps. At each statue, each figure carved in a relief or on a column, the teacher supplies some facts and then invariably adds, "We don't know what it means."

Here is a *chac-mool*, a very popular kind of statue: a human figure, half-reclining, holds a tray; on this tray – the experts are unanimous in saying – the bleeding hearts of the victims of human sacrifice were presented. These statues in and of themselves could also be seen as good-natured, rough puppets; but every time Mr Palomar sees one he cannot help shuddering.

The line of schoolboys passes. And the teacher is saying, "*Esto es un chac-mool. No se sabe lo quiere decir*," and he moves on.

Though Mr Palomar continues to follow the explanation of his friend acting as guide, he always ends up crossing the path of the schoolboys and overhearing the teacher's words. He is fascinated by his friend's wealth of mythological references: the play of interpretation, allegorical readings, have always seemed to him a supreme exercise of the mind. But

he feels attracted also by the opposite attitude of the
schoolteacher: what had at first seemed only a brisk lack of
interest is being revealed to him as a scholarly and pedagogical
position, a methodological choice by this serious and con-
scientious young man, a rule from which he will not swerve.
A stone, a figure, a sign, a word that reach us isolated from
its context is only that stone, figure, sign or word: we can
try to define them, to describe them as they are, and no
more than that; whether, beside the face they show us,
they also have a hidden face, it is not for us to know. The
refusal to comprehend more than what the stones show us
is perhaps the only way to evince respect for their secret;
trying to guess is a presumption, a betrayal of that true,
lost meaning.

Behind the pyramid there is a passage or communication
trench between two walls, one of packed earth, the other of
carved stone: the Wall of the Serpents. It is perhaps the most
beautiful piece in Tula: in the relief-frieze there is a sequence
of serpents, each holding a human skull in its open jaws, as if
it were about to devour it.

The boys go by. The teacher says, "This is the wall of the
serpents. Each serpent has a skull in its mouth. We don't
know what they mean."

Mr Palomar's friend cannot contain himself: "Yes, we
do! It's the continuity of life and death; the serpents are
life, the skulls are death. Life is life because it bears death
with it, and death is death because there is no life without
death . . ."

The boys listen, mouths agape, black eyes dazed. Mr
Palomar thinks that every translation requires another translation and so on. He asks himself, "What did death, life,
continuity, passage mean for the ancient Toltecs? And what
can they mean today for these boys? And for me?" And yet
he knows he could never suppress in himself the need to
translate, to move from one language to another, from concrete figures to abstract words, to weave and re-weave a

network of analogies. Not to interpret is impossible, as refraining from thinking is impossible. Once the school group has disappeared around a corner, the stubborn voice of the little teacher resumes: "*No es verdad*, it is not true, what that *señor* said. We don't know what they mean."

The odd slipper

While traveling in an eastern country, Mr Palomar bought a pair of slippers in a bazaar. Returning home, he tries to put them on: he realizes that one slipper is wider than the other and will not stay on his foot. He recalls the old vendor crouched on his heels in a niche of the bazaar in front of a pile of slippers of every size, at random; he sees the man as he rummages in the pile to find a slipper suited to the customer's foot, has him try it on, then starts rummaging again to hand him the presumed mate, which Mr Palomar accepts without trying it on.

"Perhaps now," Mr Palomar thinks, "another man is walking around that country with a mismated pair of slippers." And he sees a slender shadow moving over the desert with a limp, a slipper falling off his foot at every step, or else, too tight, imprisoning a twisted foot. "Perhaps he, too, at this moment is thinking of me, hoping to run into me and make the trade. The relationship binding us is more concrete and clear than many of the relationships established between human beings. And yet we will never meet." He decides to go on wearing these odd slippers out of solidarity towards his unknown companion in misfortune, to keep alive this complementary relationship that is so rare, this mirroring of limping steps from one continent to another.

He lingers over this image, but he knows it does not

correspond to the truth. An avalanche of slippers, sewn on an assembly-line, comes periodically to top up the old merchant's pile in a bazaar. At the bottom of the pile there will always remain two odd slippers, but until the old merchant exhausts his supply (and perhaps he will never exhaust it, and after his death the shop with all its merchandise will pass to his heirs and to the heirs of his heirs), it will suffice to search in the pile and one slipper will always be found to match another slipper. A mistake can occur only with an absent-minded customer like himself, but centuries can go by before the consequences of this mistake affect another visitor to that ancient bazaar. Every process of disintegration in the order of the world is irreversible; the effects, however, are hidden and delayed by the dust-cloud of the great numbers, which contains virtually limitless possibilities of new symmetries, combinations, pairings.

But what if his mistake had simply erased an earlier mistake? What if his absent-mindedness had been the bearer not of disorder but of order? "Perhaps the merchant knew what he was doing," Mr Palomar thinks. "In giving me that mismated slipper, he was righting a disparity that had been hidden for centuries in that pile of slippers, handed down from generation to generation in that bazaar."

The unknown companion was limping perhaps in another period, the symmetry of their steps responded not only from one continent to another but over a distance of centuries. This does not make Mr Palomar feel less solidarity with him. He goes on shuffling awkwardly, to afford relief to his shadow.

PALOMAR IN SOCIETY

On biting the tongue

In a time and in a country where everyone goes out of his way to announce opinions or hand down judgements, Mr Palomar has made a habit of biting his tongue three times before asserting anything. After the bite, if he is still convinced of what he was going to say, he says it. If not, he keeps his mouth shut. In fact, he spends whole weeks, months in silence.

Good opportunities for keeping quiet are never in short supply, but there are also rare occasions when Mr Palomar regrets not having said something he could have said at the right moment. He realizes that events have confirmed what he was thinking and if he had expressed his thoughts at the time, he would have had a positive influence, however slight, on what then ensued. In these cases his spirit is torn between self-satisfaction for having seen things properly and a sense of guilt because of his excessive reserve. Both feelings are so strong that he is tempted to put them into words; but after having bitten his tongue three times, or rather six, he is convinced he has no cause either for pride or for remorse.

Having had the correct view is nothing meritorious: statistically, it is almost inevitable that among the many cockeyed, confused or banal ideas that come into his mind, there should also be some perspicacious ideas, even ideas of genius; and as they occurred to him, they can surely have occurred also to somebody else.

Opinion on his having refrained from expressing his idea is more open to debate. In times of general silence, conforming to the silence of the majority is certainly culpable. In times when everybody says too much, the important thing is not merely to say what is right, which in any event would be lost in the flood of words, but to say it on the basis of premisses, suggesting also consequences, so that what is said acquires the maximum value. But then, if the value of a single affirmation lies in the continuity and coherence of the discourse in which it is uttered, the only possible choice is between speaking continuously or never speaking at all. In the first case Mr Palomar would reveal that his thinking does not proceed in a straight line but zigzags its way through vacillations, denials, corrections, in whose midst the rightness of that affirmation of his would be lost. As for the other alternative, it implies an art of keeping silent even more difficult than the art of speaking.

In fact, silence can also be considered a kind of speech, since it is a rejection of the use to which others put words; but the meaning of this silent speech lies in its interruptions, in what is, from time to time, actually said, giving a meaning to what is unsaid.

Or rather: a silence can serve to dismiss certain words or else to hold them in reserve for use on a better occasion. Just as a word spoken now can save a hundred words tomorrow or else can necessitate the saying of another thousand. "Every time I bite my tongue," Mr Palomar concludes mentally, "I must think not only of what I am about to say or not say, but also of everything that, whether I say it or do not say it, will be said or not said by me or by others." Having formulated this thought, he bites his tongue and remains silent.

On becoming angry with the young

In a time when young people's impatience with the old and old people's impatience with the young has reached its peak, when the old do nothing but store up arguments with which to tell the young finally what they deserve, and when the young are waiting only for these occasions in order to show the old that they understand nothing, Mr Palomar is unable to utter a word. If he sometimes tries to speak up, he realizes that all are too intent on the theses they are defending to pay any attention to what he is trying to clarify to himself.

The fact is that he would like not so much to affirm a truth of his own as to ask questions, and he realizes that no one wants to abandon the train of his own discourse to answer questions that, coming from another discourse, would necessitate rethinking the same things with other words, perhaps ending up on strange ground, far from safe paths. Or else he would like others to ask him questions; but he, too, would want only certain questions and not others: the ones to which he would answer by saying the things he feels he can say but could say only if someone asked him to say them. In any event, nobody has the slightest idea of asking him anything.

In this situation Mr Palomar confines himself to brooding privately on the difficulty of speaking to the young.

He thinks: "The difficulty lies in the fact that between us and them there is an unbridgeable gap. Something has happened between our generation and theirs, a continuity of experience has been broken: we no longer have any common reference points."

Then he thinks: "No, the difficulty lies in the fact that every time I am about to reproach or criticize or exhort or advise them, I think that as a young man I also attracted reproaches, criticism, exhortation, advice of the same sort, and I never listened to any of it. Times were different and as a result there were many differences in behavior, language, customs; but my mental processes then were not very different from theirs today. So I have no authority to speak."

Mr Palomar vacillates at length between these two views of the question. Then he decides: "There is no contradiction between the two positions. The break between the generations derives from the impossibility of transmitting experience, of saving others from making the mistakes we have already made. The real distance between two generations is created by the elements they have in common, that require the cyclical repetition of the same experiences, as in the behavior of animal species, handed down through biological heredity. The elements of real difference between us and them are, on the contrary, the result of the irreversible changes that every period evolves; these differences are the result of the historical legacy that we have handed on to them, the true legacy for which we are responsible, even if unconsciously sometimes. This is why we have nothing to teach: we can exert no influence on what most resembles our own experience; in what bears our own imprint we are unable to recognize ourselves."

The model of models

In Mr Palomar's life there was a period when his rule was this: first, to construct in his mind a model, the most perfect, logical, geometrical model possible; second, to see if the model is adapted to the practical situations observed in experience; third, to make the corrections necessary for model and reality to coincide. This procedure, developed by physicists and astronomers, who investigate the structure of matter and of the universe, seemed to Palomar the only way to tackle the most entangled human problems, those involving society, first of all, and the best way to govern. He had to be able to bear in mind, on the one hand, the shapeless and senseless reality of human society, which does nothing but generate monstrosities and disasters; and, on the other hand, a model of the perfect social organism, designed with neatly drawn lines, straight or circular or elliptical, parallelograms of forms, diagrams with abscissas and ordinates.

To construct a model – as Palomar was aware – you have to start with something; that is, you have to have principles, from which, by deduction, you achieve your own line of reasoning. These principles, also known as axioms or postulates, are not something you select; you have them already, because if you did not have them, you could not even begin thinking. So Palomar also had some, but since he was neither a mathematician nor a logician he did not bother to define them. Deduction, in any case, was one of his favorite activities, because he could devote himself to it in silence and alone, without special equipment, at any place and moment, seated in his armchair or strolling. Induction, on the contrary, was something he somewhat distrusted, perhaps because his experiences of it seemed vague and incomplete. The construction of a model, therefore, was for him a miracle of equilibrium between principles (left in shadow) and experience (elusive), but the result should be more substantial than either. In a well-made model, in fact, every detail must be conditioned by the others, so that everything holds together in absolute coherence, as in a mechanism where if one gear jams, everything jams. A model is by definition that in which nothing has to be changed, that which works perfectly; whereas reality, as we see clearly, does not work and constantly falls to pieces; so we must force it, more or less roughly, to assume the form of the model.

For a long time Mr Palomar made an effort to achieve such impassiveness and detachment that what counted was only the serene harmony of the lines of the pattern: all the lacerations and contortions and compressions that human reality has to undergo to conform to the model were to be considered transitory, irrelevant accidents. But if for a moment he stopped gazing at the harmonious geometrical design drawn in the heaven of ideal models, a human landscape leaped to his eye where monstrosities and disasters had not vanished at all and the lines of the design seemed distorted and twisted.

A delicate job of adjustment was then required, making gradual corrections in the model, so it would approach a possible reality, and in reality to make it approach the model. In fact, the degree of pliability in human nature is not unlimited, as he first believed; and, at the same time, even the most rigid model can show some unexpected elasticity. In other words, if the model does not succeed in transforming reality, reality must succeed in transforming the model

Mr Palomar's rule had gradually altered: now he needed a great variety of models, perhaps interchangeable, in a combining process, in order to find the one that would best fit a reality that, for its own part, was always made of many different realities, in time and in space.

In all this period, Palomar did not develop models himself or try to apply those already developed: he confined himself to imagine a right use of the right models to bridge the gap that he saw yawning, ever wider, between reality and principles. In other words, the way in which models could be managed and manipulated was not his responsibility nor was it in his power to intervene. People who concerned themselves with these things were usually quite different from him. They judged the models' functionality by other criteria: as instruments of power especially, rather than according to principles or to consequences. This attitude was fairly natural, since what the models seek to model is basically always a system of power; but if the efficacy of the system is measured by its invulnerability and capacity to last, the model becomes a kind of fortress whose thick walls conceal what is outside. Palomar, who from powers and counter-powers expects always the worst, was finally convinced that what really counts is what happens *despite* them: the form that society is assuming slowly, silently, anonymously, in people's habits, their way of thinking and acting, in their scale of values. If this is how things stand, the model of models Palomar dreams of must serve to achieve transparent models, diaphanous, fine as cobwebs, or perhaps even to dissolve models, or indeed to dissolve itself.

At this point the only thing Palomar can do was erase from his mind all models and the models of models. When this step is also taken, then he finds himself face to face with reality – hard to master and impossible to homogenize – as he formulates his "yesses" and his "noes", his "buts". To do this, it is better for the mind to remain cleared, furnished only by the memory of fragments of experience and of

principles understood and not demonstrable. This is not a
line of conduct from which he can derive special satisfaction,
but it is the only one that proves practicable for him.

As long as it is a matter of demonstrating the ills of society
and the abuses of those who abuse, he has no hesitations
(except for the fear that, if they are talked about too much,
even the most just propositions can sound repetitive,
obvious, tired). He finds it more difficult to say something
about the remedies, because first he would like to make sure
they do not cause worse ills and abuses, and that if wisely
planned by enlightened reformers, they can then be put into
practice without harm by their successors: foolish perhaps,
perhaps frauds, perhaps frauds and foolish at once.

He has only to expound these fine thoughts in a systematic
form, but a scruple restrains him: what if a model did not
result? And so he prefers to keep his convictions in the fluid
state, check them instance by instance, and make them the
implicit rule of his own everyday behavior, in doing or not
doing, in choosing or rejecting, in speaking or in remaining
silent.

THE MEDITATIONS OF PALOMAR

The world looks at the world

After a series of intellectual misadventures not worth recalling, Mr Palomar has decided that his chief activity will be looking at things from the outside. A bit nearsighted, absent-minded, introverted, he does not seem to belong temperamentally to that human type generally called an observer. And yet it has always happened that certain things – a stone wall, a seashell, a leaf, a teapot – present themselves to him as if asking him for minute and prolonged attention: he starts observing them almost unawares and his gaze begins to run over all the details, and is then unable to detach itself. Mr Palomar has decided that from now on he will redouble his attention: first, by not allowing these summons to escape him as they arrive from things; second, to attribute to the observer's operation the importance it deserves.

At this point a first critical moment arrives: sure that from now on the world will reveal an infinite wealth of things for him to look at, Mr Palomar tries staring at everything that comes within eyeshot; he feels no pleasure, and he stops. A second phase follows, in which he is convinced that only some things are to be looked at, others not, and he must go and seek the right ones. To do this, he has to face each time problems of selection, exclusion, hierarchies of preference; he soon realizes he is spoiling everything, as always when he involves his own ego and all the problems he has with his own ego.

But how can you look at something and set your own ego aside? Whose eyes are doing the looking? As a rule, you think of the ego as one who is peering out of your own eyes as if leaning on a windowsill, looking at the world stretching out before him in all its immensity. So then: there is a window that looks out on the world. The world is out there; and in here, what is there? The world still – what else could there be? With a little effort of concentration Palomar manages to shift the world from in front of him and set it on the sill, looking out. The world is also there, and for the occasion has been split into a looking world and a world looked at. And what about him, also known as "I", namely Mr Palomar? Is he not a piece of the world that is looking at another piece of world? Or else, given that there is world that side of the window and world this side, perhaps the I, the ego, is simply the window through which the world looks at the world. To look at itself the world needs the eyes (and the eyeglasses) of Mr Palomar.

So from now on Mr Palomar will look at things from outside and not from inside. But this is not enough: he will look at them with a gaze that comes from outside, not inside, himself. He tries to perform the experiment at once: now it is not he who is looking; it is the world of outside that is looking outside. Having established this, he casts his gaze around, expecting a general transfiguration. No such thing. The usual quotidian grayness surrounds him. Everything has to be rethought from the beginning. Having the outside look outside is not enough: the trajectory must start from the looked-at thing, linking it with the thing that looks.

From the mute distance of things a sign must come, a summons, a wink: one thing detaches itself from the other things with the intention of signifying something . . . What? Itself, a thing is happy to be looked at by other things only when it is convinced that it signifies itself and nothing else, amid things that signify themselves and nothing else.

Opportunities of this kind are not frequent, to be sure; but sooner or later they will have to arise: it is enough to wait for one of those lucky coincidences to occur when the world wants to look and be looked at in the same instant and Mr Palomar happens to be going by. Or rather, Mr Palomar does not even have to wait, because these things happen only when you are not awaiting them.

The universe as mirror

Mr Palomar suffers greatly because of his difficulty in establishing relations with his fellow-man. He envies those people who have the gift of always finding the right thing to say, the right greeting for everyone, people who are at ease with anyone they happen to encounter and put others at their ease; who move easily among people and immediately understand when they must defend themselves and keep their distance or when they can win trust and affection; who give their best in their relations with others and make others want to give their best; who know at once how to evaluate a person with regard to themselves and on an absolute scale.

"These gifts," Palomar thinks with the regret of the man who lacks them, "are granted to those who live in harmony with the world. It is natural for them to establish an accord not only with people but also with things, places, situations, occasions, with the course of the constellations in the firmament, with the association of atoms in molecules. That avalanche of simultaneous events that we call the universe does not overwhelm the lucky individual who can slip through the finest interstices among the infinite combinations, permutations and chains of consequences, avoiding the paths of the murderous meteorites and catching only the beneficent rays. To the man who is the friend of the universe, the universe is a friend. "If only," Palomar sighs, "I could be like that!"

He decides to try to imitate such people. All his efforts, from now on, will be directed towards achieving a harmony both with the human race, his neighbor, and with the most distant spiral of the system of the galaxies. To begin with, since his neighbor has too many problems, Palomar will try to improve his relations with the universe. He avoids and reduces to a minimum his association with his similars; he becomes accustomed to making his mind a blank, expelling all indiscreet presences; he observes the sky on starry nights; he reads books on astronomy; he becomes familiar with the notion of sidereal spaces until this becomes a permanent item in his mental furniture. Then he tries to make his thoughts retain simultaneously the nearest things and the farthest: when he lights his pipe he is intent on the flame of the match that at his next puff should allow itself to be drawn to the bottom of the bowl, initiating the slow transformation of shreds of tobacco into embers; but this attention must not make him forget even for a moment the explosion of a supernova taking place in the great Magellanic Cloud at this same instant, that is to say a few million years ago. The idea that everything in the universe is connected and corresponds never leaves him: a variation in the luminosity in the Nebula of Cancer or the condensation of a globular mass in Andromeda cannot help but have some influence on the functioning of his record-player or on the freshness of the watercress leaves in his bowl of salad.

When he is convinced that he has precisely outlined his own place in the midst of the silent expanse of things floating in the void, amid the dust-cloud of present or possible events that hovers in space and time, Palomar decides the moment has come to apply this cosmic wisdom to relations with his fellows. He hastens to return to society, renews acquaintances, friendships, business associations; he subjects his ties and affections to a careful examination of conscience. He expects to see, extending before him, a human landscape that is finally distinct, clear, without mists, where he will be able to move

with precise and confident gestures. Is this what happens? Not
at all. He starts by becoming embroiled in a muddle of
misunderstandings, hesitations, compromises, failures to act;
the most futile matters stir up anguish, the most serious
become unimportant; everything he says or does proves
clumsy, jarring, irresolute. What is it that does not work?

This: contemplating the stars he has become accustomed to
considering himself an anonymous and incorporeal dot,
almost forgetting that he exists; to deal now with human
beings he cannot help involving himself, and he no longer
knows where his self is to be found. In dealing with every
person one should know where to place himself with regard
to that person, should be sure of the reaction the presence of
the other inspires in him – dislike or attraction, dominion or
subjugation, discipleship or mastery, performance as actor or
as spectator – and on the basis of these and their counter-
reactions one should then establish the rules of the game to
be applied in their play, the moves and counter-moves to be
made. But for all this, even before he starts observing the
others, one should know well who he is himself. Knowledge
of one's fellow has this special aspect: it passes necessarily
through knowledge of oneself; and this is precisely what
Palomar is lacking. Not only knowledge is needed, but also
comprehension, agreement with one's own means and ends
and impulses, which is like saying the possibility of exercis-
ing a mastery over one's own inclinations and actions that
will control them and direct them but not coerce them or
stifle them. The people he admires for the rightness and
naturalness of their every word and every action are not only
at peace with the universe but, first of all, at peace with
themselves. Palomar, who does not love himself, has always
taken care not to encounter himself face to face; this is why he
preferred to take refuge among the galaxies; now he understands that he should have begun by finding an inner peace.
The universe can perhaps go tranquilly about its business; he
surely cannot.

The road left open to him is this: he will devote himself
from now on to the knowing of himself, he will explore his
own inner geography, he will draw the diagram of the
moods of his spirit, he will derive from it formulas and
theories, he will train his telescope on the orbits traced by the
course of his life rather than on those of the constellations.
"We can know nothing about what is outside us, if we
overlook ourselves," he thinks now, "the universe is the
mirror in which we can contemplate only what we have
learned to know in ourselves."

And thus this new phase of his itinerary in search of
wisdom is also achieved. Finally his gaze can rove freely
inside himself. What will he see? Will his inner world seem to
him an immense, calm rotation of a luminous spiral? Will he
see stars and planets navigating in silence on the parabolas
and ellipses that determine character and destiny? Will he
contemplate a sphere of infinite circumference that has the
ego as its center and its center in every point?

He opens his eyes. What appears to his gaze is something
he seems to have seen already, every day: streets full of
people, hurrying, elbowing their way ahead, without looking one another in the face, among high walls, sharp and
peeling. In the background, the starry sky scatters intermittent flashes like a stalled mechanism, which jerks and creaks
in all its unoiled joints, outposts of an endangered universe,
twisted, restless as he is.

Learning to be dead

Mr Palomar decides that from now on he will act as if he were dead, to see how the world gets along without him. For some while he has realized that things between him and the world are no longer proceeding as they did before; before, they seemed to expect something, one of the other, he and the world, now he no longer recalls what there was to expect, good or bad, or why this expectation kept him in a perpetually agitated, anxious state.

So now Mr Palomar should feel a sensation of relief, no longer having to wonder what the world has in store for him; and there should be relief also for the world, which no longer has to bother about him. But it is the very expectation of enjoying this calm that makes Mr Palomar anxious.

In other words, being dead is less easy than it might seem. First of all, you must not confuse being dead with not being, a condition that occupies the vast expanse of time before birth, apparently symmetrical with the other, equally vast expanse that follows death. In fact, before birth we are part of the infinite possibilities that may or may not be fulfilled; whereas, once dead, we cannot fulfill ourselves either in the past (to which we now belong entirely but on which we can no longer have any influence) or in the future (which, even if influenced by us, remains forbidden to us). Mr Palomar's case is really more simple, since his capacity for having an influence on anything or anybody has always been negligible: the world can very well do without him, and he can consider himself dead quite serenely, without even altering his habits. The problem is not the change in what he does but in what he is, or more specifically in what he is as far as the world is concerned. Before, by "world" he meant the world plus himself; now it is a question of himself plus the world minus him.

Does the world minus him mean an end to anxiety? A world in which things happen independently of his presence and his reactions, following a law of their own or a necessity or rationale that does not involve him? The wave strikes the cliff and hollows out the rock, another wave arrives, another, and still another; whether he is or is not, everything goes on happening. The relief in being dead should be this: having eliminated that patch of uneasiness that is our presence, the only thing that matters is the extension and succession of things under the sun, in their impassive serenity. All is calm or tends towards calm, even hurricanes, earthquakes, the eruption of volcanoes. But was this not the earlier world, when he was in it? When every storm bore within itself the peace of afterwards, prepared the moment when all the waves would have struck the shore, and the wind will have spent its force? Perhaps being dead is passing into the ocean of the waves that remain waves forever, so it is futile to wait for the sea to become calm.

The gaze of the dead is always a bit deprecatory. Places, situations, occasions are more or less what one already knew, and recognizing them always affords a certain satisfaction; but at the same time many variations, large and small, become noticeable. In and of themselves they could be acceptable, too, if they corresponded to a logical, coherent process; but instead they prove arbitrary and irregular, and this is irksome, especially because one is always tempted to intervene and make the correction that seems necessary, and being dead, one cannot do it. Hence an attitude of reluctance, almost of embarrassment, but at the same time of smugness, the attitude of one who knows that what counts is his own past experience and there is no point in attaching too much importance to all the rest. Then a dominant feeling is quick to arise and impose itself on every thought: it is the relief of knowing that all those problems are other people's problems, their business. The dead should no longer give a damn about anything because it is not up to them to think about it any more; and even if that may seem immoral, it is in this irresponsibility that the dead find their gaiety.

The more Mr Palomar's spiritual condition approaches the one here described, the more the idea of being dead seems natural to him. To be sure, he has not yet found the sublime detachment he thought was usual with the dead, nor a reason that surpasses all explanation, nor an emergence from his own confines like emerging from a tunnel that opens out into other dimensions. At times he has the illusion of being freed at least from the impatience he has felt all his life on seeing others get everything they do wrong and in thinking that in their place he would get it all equally wrong but would at least be aware of his errors. But he is not in the least freed of this impatience, and he realizes that his intolerence of the others' mistakes and of his own will be perpetuated along with those mistakes, which no death can erase. So he might as well get used to it: for Palomar, being dead means resigning himself to the disappointment in finding himself the same in a definitive state, which he can no longer hope to change.

Palomar does not underestimate the advantages that the condition of being alive can have over that of being dead: not as regards the future, where risks are always very great and benefits can be of short duration, but in the sense of the possibility of improving the form of one's own past. (Unless one is already fully satisfied with one's own past, a situation too uninteresting to make it worth investigating.) A person's life consists of a collection of events, the last of which could also change the meaning of the whole, not because it counts more than the previous ones but because once they are included in a life, events are arranged in an order that is not chronological but rather corresponds to an inner architecture. A person, for example, reads in adulthood a book that is important for him, and it makes him say, "How could I have lived without having read it!" and also, "What a pity I did not read it in my youth!" Well, these statements do not have much meaning, especially the second, because after he has read that book, his life becomes the life of a person who has read that book, and it is of little importance whether he read it early or late, because now his life before that reading also assumes a form shaped by that reading.

This is the most difficult step for one who wants to learn how to be dead: convincing himself that his own life is a closed whole, all in the past, to which nothing can be added, nor can changes in perspective be introduced in the relationships among the various elements. Of course, those who go on living can, according to the changes they experience, introduce changes also in the lives of the dead, giving form to what had none or what seemed to have a different form: recognizing, for example, a just rebel in someone who had been vituperated for his actions against the law, celebrating a poet or a prophet in one who had felt himself sentenced to neurosis or delirium. But these are changes that matter mostly for the living. It is unlikely that they, the dead, will profit by them. Each individual is made up of what he has lived and the way he lived it, and no one can take this away from him. Anyone who has lived in suffering is always made of that suffering; if they try to take it away from him, he is no longer himself.

Therefore Palomar prepares to become a grouchy dead man, reluctant to submit to the sentence to remain exactly as he is; but he is unwilling to give up anything of himself, even if it is a burden.

Of course, it is also possible to rely on those alternatives that guarantee survival of at least a part of the self in posterity. These views can be divided into two broad categories: the biological mechanism, which allows leaving descendants that part of the self known as the genetic heritage; and the historical mechanism, which grants a continuance in the memory and language of those who go on living and inherit that portion, large or small, of experience that even the most inept man gathers and stores up. These mechanisms can also be seen as a single one, considering the succession of generations like the stages in the life of a single person, which goes on for centuries and millenia; but this is simply a postponement of the problem, from one's own individual death to the extinction of the human race, however late this may occur.

Thinking of his own death, Palomar already thinks of that of the last survivors of the human species or of its derivations or heirs. On the terrestrial globe, devastated and deserted, explorers from another planet land; they decipher the clues recorded in the hieroglyphics of the pyramids and in the punched cards of the electronic calculators; the memory of the human race is reborn from its ashes and is spread through the inhabited zones of the universe. And so, after one post-ponement or another, the moment comes when it is time to wear out and be extinguished in an empty sky, when the last material evidence of the memory of living will degenerate in a flash of heat, or will crystallize its atoms in the chill of an immobile order.

"If time has to end, it can be described, instant by instant,"

Palomar thinks, "and each instant, when described, expands so that its end can no longer be seen." He decides that he will set himself to describing every instant of his life, and until he has described them all he will no longer think of being dead. At that moment he dies.

INDEX

The numbers 1, 2, 3 that mark the titles of the index, whether they are in the first, second, or third position, besides having a purely ordinal value, correspond also to three thematic areas, three kinds of experience and enquiry that, in varying proportions, are present in every part of the book.

Those marked 1 generally correspond to a visual experience, whose object is almost always some natural form; the text tends to belong to a descriptive category.

Those marked 2 contain anthropological elements, or cultural in the broad sense; and the experience involves, besides visual data, also language, meaning, symbols. The text tends to take the form of a story.

Those marked 3 involve more speculative experience, concerning the cosmos, time, infinity, the relationship between the self and the world, the dimensions of the mind. From the confines of description and narrative we move into the area of meditation.

Italo Calvino
Invisible Cities £2.50

'This most beautiful of all his books throws up ideas, allusions, and breath-taking imaginative, insights on almost every page. Each time he returns from his travels, Marco Polo is invited by Kublai Khan to describe the cities he has visited. The conqueror and explorer exchange visions. for Kublai Khan the world is constantly expanding, for Marco Polo, who has seen so much of it, it is an ever-diminishing place Calvino is describing only one city in this book Venice, that decaying heap of incomparable splen-dour, still stands as substantial evidence of man's ability to create some-thing perfect out of chaos ' TIMES LITERARY SUPPLEMENT

'The cities correspond to psychological states and historical states, possi-bilities and transformations' LISTENER

If on a Winter's Night a Traveller £2.95

A fiction about fictions, a novel about novels, a book about books Its chief protagonists are its author and his reader. Its progress traces the reading of a novel and the consummation of a love affair. In its course a whole shelf of novels are begun and – for reasons at the time entirely reasonable – never finished. Its characters are the myriads of beings involved with the process of creation, construction and consumption of The Book

'I can think of no finer writer to have beside me while Italy explodes, while Britain burns, while the world ends'
SALMAN RUSHDIE, LONDON REVIEW OF BOOKS

Umberto Eco
Name of the Rose £3.95

'Imagine a medieval castle run by the Benedictines, with cellarists, herbalists, gardeners, novices. One after another, half a dozen monks are found murdered in bizarre ways. A learned Franciscan who is sent to solve the mystery finds himself involved in the frightening events . . . a sleuth's pursuit of the truth behind the mystery also involves the pursuit of meaning – in words, symbols, ideas, every conceivable sign'
NEW YORK TIMES BOOK REVIEW

'The most intelligent – and at the same time the most amusing – book in years' DER SPIEGEL

Intellectual delight and all the excitement of a tremendous climax enough for any thriller' BOOKS and BOOKMEN

'Belongs with Voltaire's philosophical tales . . . an erudite fiction story, it is also a vibrant plea for freedom, moderation and wisdom' L'EXPRESS

Ellen Gilchrist
In the Land of Dreamy Dreams £2.50

'Most of the girls in Ellen Gilchrist's dreamscapes live in New Orleans. Her subjects include murder, suicide and abortion, and her characters are full of fear, fear of the dark, of the unknown, of the future' LISTENER

'A sustained display of delicately and rhythmically modulated prose and an unsentimental dissection of raw sentiment'
THE TIMES LITERARY SUPPLEMENT

'Gilchrist's stories are elegant little tragedies, memorable and cruel. Her sketches of adolescent torments prompt comparison with Carson McCullers. Her fading desperate ladies are close cousins to Blanche Dubois and Mrs Stone' THE TIMES

Picador

☐	**Burning Leaves**	Don Bannister	£2.50p
☐	**Making Love: The Picador Book of Erotic Verse**	edited by Alan Bold	£1.95p
☐	**Bury My Heart at Wounded Knee**	Dee Brown	£4.50p
☐	**Cities of the Red Night**	William Burroughs	£2.50p
☐	**The Road to Oxiana**	Robert Byron	£2.95p
☐	**If on a Winter's Night a Traveller**	Italo Calvino	£2.95p
☐	**Auto Da Fé**	Elias Canetti	£3.95p
☐	**Exotic Pleasures**	Peter Carey	£1.95p
☐	**Chandler Collection Vol. 1**	Raymond Chandler	£4.95p
☐	**In Patagonia**	Bruce Chatwin	£2.75p
☐	**Crown Jewel**	Ralph de Boissiere	£2.75p
☐	**Letters from Africa 1914—1931**	Isak Dinesen (Karen Blixen)	£3.95p
☐	**The Book of Daniel**	E. L. Doctorow	£2.95p
☐	**Debts of Honour**	Michael Foot	£2.50p
☐	**One Hundred Years of Solitude**	Gabriel García Márquez	£3.50p
☐	**Nothing, Doting, Blindness**	Henry Green	£2.95p
☐	**The Obstacle Race**	Germaine Greer	£6.95p
☐	**Roots**	Alex Haley	£4.95p
☐	**The Four Great Novels**	Dashiel Hammett	£5.95p
☐	**When the Tree Sings**	Stratis Haviaras	£1.95p
☐	**Dispatches**	Michael Herr	£2.75p
☐	**Riddley Walker**	Russell Hoban	£2.75p
☐	**Three Trapped Tigers**	C. Cabrera Infante	£2.95p
☐	**Unreliable Memoirs**	Clive James	£2.50p
☐	**Man and His Symbols**	Carl Jung	£3.95p
☐	**China Men**	Maxine Hong Kingston	£2.95p
☐	**Janus: A Summing Up**	Arthur Koestler	£3.50p
☐	**Memoirs of a Survivor**	Doris Lessing	£2.95p
☐	**Albert Camus**	Herbert Lottman	£3.95p
☐	**Zany Afternoons**	Bruce McCall	£4.95p
☐	**The Cement Garden**	Ian McEwan	£2.50p
☐	**The Serial**	Cyra McFadden	£1.75p
☐	**McCarthy's List**	Mary Mackey	£1.95p
☐	**Daddyji/Mamaji**	Ved Mehta	£3.50p
☐	**Slowly Down the Ganges**	Eric Newby	£2.95p
☐	**The Snow Leopard**	Peter Matthiessen	£3.50p

☐	**Lectures on Literature**	Vladimir Nabokov	£3.95p
☐	**The Best of Myles**	Flann O' Brien	£3.50p
☐	**Autobiography**	John Cowper Powys	£3.50p
☐	**Hadrian the Seventh**	Fr. Rolfe (Baron Corvo)	£1.25p
☐	**On Broadway**	Damon Runyon	£3.95p
☐	**Midnight's Children**	Salman Rushdie	£3.95p
☐	**Awakenings**	Oliver Sacks	£3.95p
☐	**The Fate of the Earth**	Jonathan Schell	£2.50p
☐	**Street of Crocodiles**	Bruno Schultz	£1.25p
☐	**Poets in their Youth**	Eileen Simpson	£2.95p
☐	**Miss Silver's Past**	Josef Skvorecky	£2.50p
☐	**A Flag for Sunrise**	Robert Stone	£2.50p
☐	**Visitants**	Randolph Stow	£2.50p
☐	**Alice Fell**	Emma Tennant	£1.95p
☐	**The Flute-Player**	D. M. Thomas	£2.50p
☐	**The Great Shark Hunt**	Hunter S. Thompson	£4.95p
☐	**The Longest War**	Jacob Timerman	£2.50p
☐	**Aunt Julia and the Scriptwriter**	Mario Vargas Llosa	£2.95p
☐	**Female Friends**	Fay Weldon	£2.95p
☐	**No Particular Place To Go**	Hugo Williams	£1.95p
☐	**The Outsider**	Colin Wilson	£3.50p
☐	**Mars**	Fritz Zorn	£1.95p

All these books are available at your local bookshop or newsagent, or can be ordered direct from the publisher. Indicate the number of copies required and fill in the form below

12

....

Name_____
(Block letters please)

Address_____

_____

Send to CS Department, Pan Books Ltd, PO Box 40, Basingstoke, Hants
Please enclose remittance to the value of the cover price plus:
35p for the first book plus 15p per copy for each additional book ordered
to a maximum charge of £1.25 to cover postage and packing
Applicable only in the UK

While every effort is made to keep prices low, it is sometimes
necessary to increase prices at short notice. Pan Books reserve
the right to show on covers and charge new retail prices which
may differ from those advertised in the text or elsewhere